HELLCAT'S BOUNTY

Renae Jones

HELLCAT'S BOUNTY

Cover design by Kanaxa

Dedication

For Laurie, with a pound of snark and an ounce of love. I knew my first self-pub would be dedicated to you, even before I knew it would be this one.

ONE

There was a saloon with no name on a forgotten space station, across from an industrial spaceport, at the back of a dirty promenade, through a real wood door. Anelace sauntered in at high noon.

She wasn't there for a drink. She was looking for a particular kind of criminal. Anelace was a freelance exterminator and her vice was money. She wanted to be back in the abandoned wilds, killing verminous blobs and earning more of it.

Around her, the No Name's decor was classic saloon. Dark wood and brass were bolted together in thick wooden chairs, backless stools, a long scuffed bar and two dozen tables. The lights were high and plentiful, little stained glass balls casting multi-colored glows. And the liquor behind the bartender was a serious display, giant bottles of whiskey and gin stacked together like choirboys before the service.

The lunch rush was just winding down. A few diners, a few more uncleared tables, and the obligatory daytime drunks littered the room. No one looked twice at the exhausted woman still carrying her weapons, still sweaty and battered from a morning of hard work.

Anelace needed a quick patch up, some fake skin on her scuffs, a little jellyfish ointment on her goo burns, and she needed it off the record. She was there to see her favorite off-the-record doctor—a woman with some self-taught medical knowledge and a good supply case.

Meidani, the doc she was looking for, stood beside a dirty table with a dish bin in her hands. She was a delicate woman with long black hair, a heart-shaped face, and wide features hinting at a second-wave ancestry. Her manner was reserved, her smile gentle, and her eyes perpetually dreamy.

She was talking to a young man made of elbows and aw-shucks. He was probably twenty-five, but he looked twelve to Anelace.

Anelace recognized the guy. She distinctly remembered Meidani turning her eyes to get a second look at him on the promenade.

Meidani didn't seem to date much lately, heading home every night to the quarters she shared with her family. But Anelace would bet hard credits the woman had an itchy libido hidden under about four layers of her propriety.

She couldn't volunteer to scratch that itch herself—Meidani was a certifiable good girl, former teacher's pet and law-abiding citizen. The one time Anelace had tried hitting on her, she'd given her a look like slime mold had started talking. They'd been in primary school at the time.

But friends didn't let friends spend their entire lives between home and work. Meidani deserved to have a good time, and if Anelace couldn't give her a good time herself... She was still going to give her a good time. And this looked like opportunity.

Anelace walked closer to the pair. The kid's jeans were starched, his hands strong, and his looks clean-cut but handsome. He was too male and too young, of course, but Anelace wasn't shopping for herself. This man was exactly the sort of sincere achiever Meidani always dated, back when she did date. And he was crazy about Meidani—you could tell by his earnest lean.

Meidani caught Anelace's eye, sending a meaning-laden look her way, but what did it mean? Expectation? Pleading?

"Howdy. How ya doing?" Anelace tipped her hat at them both, a mannish gesture she loved for the contrast with her feminine long hair and not half-bad rack.

"Howdy," the admirer nodded.

"Hi, Anelace." Meidani's greeting was warmer.

Anelace might have known the kid's name, but she couldn't remember it. So she bluffed her way through, clapping him on the shoulder in a neighborly way. "And how've you been? How's your family?"

Everyone on Rosewood had a family, right?

The kid's grin was genuine. "I'm doing good. My sister had a baby. She's doing good too. And the baby looks just like me."

"The poor baby," Anelace said mournfully, confusing him and making Meidani laugh. "No, I'm just kidding you. Have you been helping out? Being the good brother?"

"Of course I have. The baby cries more than anything , but he'll smile for me."

Meidani was smiling at him, too. A good sign.

"A charmer, then," Anelace said.

The kid nodded over-eager agreement, for a little too long, like he hadn't understood her. When he realized both of the women were looking at him, he coughed and faced Meidani again. "So, I was about to ask, why aren't you a waitress yet? You'd be great at it."

He made the last bit encouraging—and patronizing.

Really? Anelace had handed him the perfect opening to present his "fine upstanding citizen" credentials and he'd blown it, preferring to gnaw on his own boot instead. Meidani wasn't a waitress because waitresses had to stand around chatting with strangers, and she was too shy to enjoy that.

"I like bussing."

She also did the books, the ordering, the hiring, and chopped the occasional stack of vegetables. Bussing, yeah.

"Okay, right. But..." The kid took a few steps closer to Meidani.

Meidani set her bin on the table, a not-so-subtle hint that went right over the kid's head.

Men couldn't flirt worth a damn. Why were straight women even straight?

Maybe this guy was too useless. But Anelace owed Meidani a favor or five, and she liked the woman. If there was any chance Meidani wanted a sweaty roll between the sheets, Anelace would help out where she could.

A momentary image of Meidani sweaty, lost in pleasure, wrapped in sheets flickered through her mind, bringing Anelace's thoughts to a stuttering halt. Heat ghosted through her body like that warm and cold feeling you got when you walked away from a bonfire. Her breath caught in her throat, turning into a cough.

Awkward.

Then Anelace dismissed the fantasy ruthlessly. That was not how their friendship worked. Anelace knew better than to imagine sexual tension with the woman who gave her free cookies and had once lectured her on the importance of cleaning her teeth after drinking alcohol.

The kid had his hat in his hands, deforming it. It was a nice hat, too—soft tan felt with a pinch in the front and a lightly flared brim.

Meidani shot a look over his bowed head, widening her eyes at Anelace. What? she seemed to be asking.

Anelace pointedly slid her gaze down to the guy's ass, the jean-filling body part she remembered Meidani checking out.

Meidani's eyes opened further, too wide for scandal and too guilty for shock. And now she was blushing.

The kid finally found a thought somewhere in his hat. "Listen, what do you like to do? After work?"

Meidani's eyes turned desperate, and she was looking right at Anelace for help. The question was too open-ended for her. She enjoyed small talk the way ship cats enjoyed baths. Until Meidani got comfortable, it was best to keep questions unobtrusive but specific.

Anelace's fingers twitched to cover the kid's mouth. Every time he spoke, he torpedoed her plans. Instead, she deflected the doomed conversation. "Hey Doc, sorry to interrupt, but I need a favor."

"Of course you do. I heard there was a bounty on," Meidani sounded aggrieved, but the tightness in her forehead softened. "How hurt are you?"

"Just a little."

"Yeah, right. Okay, just let me..." she gestured at the dish-stacked tables. "They're driving me crazy. Stuff is congealing."

"Sure thing."

When the kid moved to help Meidani, Anelace held him back. An amateur clearing tables would just slow her down and put that little tension wrinkle back between her eyes.

When the doctor slash barmaid slash busser moved to the next table, her admirer shot Anelace a calculating look, like a five-year old trying his hand at card sharping. "You're her friend, right?"

Anelace and Meidani had met in primary school. Anelace, with tangled hair and deadbeat parents, had been there but ignored lessons and counted down the time until meals. Meidani had been the opposite, a smart cookie in a pretty white dress one year older and a decade more mature.

They'd left school acquaintances, though. They met again recently when the quack doc Anelace used to see had died. Meidani had taken over his clientele of illegals, outlaws, and the paranoid.

"Yeah, I'm her friend."

"Any tips?"

The kid was twisting his hands again, fidgeting his hat between them.

"One tip: don't ruin your hat. It's a nice hat."

He chuckled feebly.

Anelace wore her own hat. It was darker brown leather, more utilitarian than the kid's hat. She'd bought it with her first big bounty take. She'd been seventeen years old with internal bleeding and recently deceased parents, but at least she'd had a nice hat.

Meidani returned from the kitchen. She was more relaxed now, and pulling off the white sackcloth apron that covered her jeans. She pointed to the back, and Anelace motioned the kid in front of her.

"Derek, it was good seeing you. Thanks for dropping by. But I need to check out Anelace's injuries. Can I finish talking to you some other time?"

Meidani dismissed the poor kid ruthlessly, in a tone sweeter than peach pie. The poor kid was shut down before he even got a chance.

Anelace was not oddly relieved. And she would not snicker.

After he was gone, Meidani led the way. "What was that about? You have a thing for Derek?"

The little storeroom where Meidani tended busted people was down a hall lit by dusty fixtures. It was small and too warm, but well lit. There were pickles and coffee and beer stacked on the left, and a cheap plastic table on the right. When you were really hurt, Meidani covered the table with a plastic sheet.

"Me? The kid? No." Anelace snorted. "What the hell would I do with him? I was just checking if you wanted to keep him. You need a date. I'm helpful like that."

Meidani thrust her hands and arms into a sanitizer and stood while it gurgled and whirred, and rolled her eyes toward the ceiling in the universal prayer for patience. "If it's the thought that counts, I'm grateful. But don't do that. Now, what happened?"

"A burn, just a dribble, on my left arm. And I cracked my leg good. Can you scan my shin, just in case?"

"Let me see. Didn't the bounty just start?"

"Five hours ago. I'm going to get some sleep and go at it again."

Meidani frowned and changed the subject. "And why a date, anyway?"

"You need to live a little," Anelace said.

"We might not have the same idea of living."

"Hey, the kid was cute."

"You tried to set me up with someone you call 'the kid'."

"I can see your point there." Anelace acknowledged.

Meidani reached for a thick tube of gold foil. Anelace had already dusted with powder, but ointment came next. It was made from little blue jellyfish, dried and ground up, and it stung like the blob had. But without it, the blob burn would never heal. The skin would grow back, but the scar would be a nerveless chunk of flesh six inches across and bone deep.

The doctor rolled the sleeve of Anelace's protective silicon-blend shirt higher. She held Anelace firmly, five gloved fingers against the sensitive skin of Anelace's wrist. Arousal caught Anelace's breath and held it hostage.

Meidani turned away, reaching for a swab, and Anelace's breath came in a woosh.

Anelace looked at the wall, hard. Lusting after her doctor's hands while she was treated? That was a new high in creepy perv. When Meidani poked the swab of ointment into the numb spot on her wrist, reigniting the fiery pain, it was a nice little break in Anelace's one-sided sexual tension.

Meidani went back to her cabinet. The storeroom felt quiet, though it wasn't. The jangling of rigged pachinko seeped from the gambling hall next door. It occurred to Anelace that Meidani spent too much time in this dusty little room.

"The kid was a poor option, but I've got one thing to say: You need to have more fun."

Meidani gave her a sideways look through thick eyelashes. "Okay. I do need to have more fun."

She agreed? That was too easy.

Meidani did the leg scan next. She ran a handheld imager, a clunky green thing meant for farm animals, over the limb. It was battered and square and shaped like a huge laser.

"It's nothing big. No fractures, no bone bruise, just the surface bruising. Not bad at all, considering your usual state. I'll put a bruise patch on it and it'll be nothing by tomorrow."

"Thank you, ma'am." Anelace reached in her pocket for credits.

"That's it?"

"That's it."

"Nothing major then." Meidani sounded relieved. She sighed, like maybe she wouldn't say it this time. But then she said it anyway. "Why do you hunt the blobs, Anelace? They'll kill you, someday."

It was a good question, but she was still coming to terms with the answer.

She'd hunted her first bounty when she was fourteen, when it was her only option, but she'd come a long way since then. The days of scrounging nutrition bars from miners, desperate to avoid company handouts that could end her on a debtor list, were past. The fear of being shipped to an asteroid work camp to pay back the company for air and food was groundless, now. She could get other work.

But she kinda thought the desperation had broken something in her. That fear would never leave her, now. She'd keep chasing money, because rock bottom still felt just a few inches away. She wasn't going to tell Meidani that.

Anelace shrugged. "Someone's gotta do it. Pays well. Why do you doctor? That could get you in some trouble, there."

It was more of a response than she'd ever given before.

Meidani opened her mouth to reply, and paused with a cute thinking wrinkle above her nose. She hadn't drawn that correlation before, and it was written on her face.

Anelace pressed money into her hand while Meidani was still thinking it out, and left before things got too deep for her.

TWO

Anelace woke languid and warm in a comfortable darkness. She lay snug in a nest of old quilts, staring up at a ceiling she couldn't see. Her wrist throbbed gently, insistently. Her body was never quiet about healing itself.

Blob burn. Right.

Anelace sat straight up, reality catching up with her mind like a mean dog on a burglar. There was a bounty on, money to be made and she was ready for round two.

She dressed, pulled back her hair, changed the bandage square on her wrist. It was an old routine for her, gearing up, reflecting on the day to come. Exterminating the carnivorous amoeba trying to take over the space station was too dangerous to just show up yawning and scratching her ass, like she had a job clerking in a shop. Hunting the man eaters—the blobs big enough to engulf a person and digest them—was even higher stakes. It was fear and adrenaline and triumph and skill and luck. She loved it.

Last step, she threw together a breakfast of sardines on toast and made the long walk down to the lowest station concourse. While she walked, she crunched through fish spines and planned her hunt.

There weren't enough people to fill the space station, a hunk of metal-encased asteroid serving as a waystation between outer asteroid fields and the Zealot Frontier proper. The Kao-Peterson Corporation, the huge mining conglomerate that built the station in the first place, had shifted its gadolinite operations twenty-some years ago, and started an exodus. And out of all the halls and sections abandoned by humanity, the bottom decks were the emptiest. Where she headed, only the blobs remained. Deadly, flesh-eating, caustic, translucent blobs.

Today was going to be a good hunt.

At the concourse, she stood in the wide entrance area to warm her stiff muscles. Her mind was alert, her aches from that morning minor. She swung her arms and rolled her neck, and stared across a metal desert devoid of life or pity, nothing left after years of scavengers and abandonment.

In front of her, a vast concourse soared eight stories up to a nearly-realistic LED sky. The area was enormous, defying the neat deck-by-deck of a space station, challenging her senses. UV-less sun beat down, remorseless on cracked stucco and concrete dust.

Large shops ringed the outer walls, forming a silent tribunal. In the center, stucco-covered buildings were offset and stacked like a giant pile of children's blocks. The stack stretched nearly to the artificial sky, tied down by suspended walkways.

It was a shame the sky didn't work in the port promenade. It was pretty, and reminded her what time it was.

A little thrill tickled her spine, her throat, and then she suppressed it. It was time to hunt, to focus, to react.

She headed in, laser in one hand, popper gun in the other.

This time she skipped the planters and headed for a steep spiraling stairway to the third floor. It would deliver her to the jumbled stack of shops in the center of the room, on the next floor up from that morning's hunt. She kicked the staircase, hard, and started a vigilant climb.

The room was quiet, of course, but louder than she'd expected. The air system was going, an unending whine in the big space, but the humidity was set low. The dry air felt too warm, and scratched at her throat. Too long down here and she'd get nosebleeds

She climbed. Blobs couldn't hear her; they sensed vibration. Wherever a gellish skin pressed, the slightest vibration would reach them. You couldn't sneak up on the things, not really, so she didn't stress every footstep.

Of course, sometimes they just ignored you. Or lay in a trap.

Two exterminators with a pitcher of beer could argue for hours about blobs, and so could scientists.

Did they derive from amoebas proper? Were they keen and vicious, or dumb buckets of jiggle? Anelace had seen both.

She reached the top of the stairs. The floor became a dusty fake marble, and there were bright blue awnings above the shops. The awnings were missing in little gaps, like an old timer's teeth, and signs hung brokenly. Worse, the shops on this row had closed doors and intact furniture. Every one was a place for blobs to hide, above a door or deep in a pile of junk.

The doors were why she preferred the lower floors or outer ring, but it wasn't a deal breaker.

Her first kill of the night was three minutes later, behind the second door. It was easily big enough to eat a cat, earning her another cool two hundred credits after multiplier.

She could buy a bottle of imported whiskey with that. She could feed herself for a month.

A smile she couldn't control if she tried stretched her face. She savored it, and moved on.

Exterminating was an odd sort of job. You had no boss, no hours, no promises. Anelace loved that part. Like scavenging, it only paid well if you risked your life. And also like scavenging, it attracted a fine mix of the biggest weirdos on the station and a few hardened professionals.

The shops ahead curved away from her, wrapped by the walkway. The nearest shop had no door, the next two were closed fast, and in the distance she thought she could see a crack in a shining grey wall.

She switched her phaser into her grip. In close quarters, she needed something with stopping power, which meant the phaser.

She skirted wide around the first doorway. The shop was filled by a jumbled mess of glass and plastic shelves, metal cross bars, the chrome facing of a counter. The wood was missing, eaten by blobs.

Right. She'd skip that one.

The automatic access on the next door was broken, or the power off. She eased it open with a loud screech of glass on metal track.

The room was bare, staring unimpressed at her gun-swiveling entrance.

Four empty shops later, she was close enough to see the shadow on the wall wasn't a crack. It was a slimy green discoloration running from floor to ceiling. It was barely an inch wide, and it scared the dickens out of her.

No blob, not a smart one, not a dumb one, would keep away from water. The drip wasn't enough to split in, but it smelled like procreation to them anyway.

She stayed light on her toes, her eyes tracing left and right, turning to keep her blind spots covered. She couldn't see water running, but the leak was enough to create mold, which made it deadly.

She turned in circles, trying to kick-start her brain.

A slight disturbance flickered along the wall far ahead, then it was gone. She kept her eyes moving, but her attention fixed, and there it was again.

A blob was coming her way, more translucent than most. As she watched, she made out a ripple against the wall, a faint shudder in the two-inch crack between shop and suspended walkway. And once she saw that, she could trace it with her eyes, and she could see it. It was squeezing up, a few inches at a time, from the floor below.

When the blob pulled its nucleus through the gap, she was waiting. She let it inch higher before firing a cranked up laser with a steady hand. She aimed for the bottleneck where it stretched thin between walkway and wall.

The laser fired in silence, shooting invisible light rays in millisecond bursts. An orange spot of light, added to help her aim, was the only sign she was firing.

She swept her aim left, along the tendril, trying for maximum damage.

The laser overheated and shut down with a cheerful chirp.

She hated lasers, and lasers hated her. Anelace cussed silently.

The blob drew up, massing into a gooey ball high on the wall. It wasn't a break for the ceiling. It just massed...

She dove to the side, twisting to get her phaser in position. The massed blob was flying for her face.

Fuck.

A phaser blast slammed the blob in midair, sending it flying fifteen feet down the walk. It hit a jiggly stop against the wall.

She charged after it.

It was stunts like that which had her half convinced these things were sentient.

Her second phaser blast pinned the blob to the wall again, pounding its hide, leaving a wide green bruise and starting some seepage.

She followed with two pressurized kerosene balls from her popper gun, though only one broke with a distinctive oily odor. Son of a bitch. It was time to refresh the propellant.

The blob sagged through the gap beside the wall, fleeing in slow motion.

She pulled out a wand. It was long bendy industrial silicone encasing an old fashioned flint. She used it to shower the area with sparks. Fire whooshed across her kill.

She waited just out of range of the merry flames, breathing through her mouth, checking her laser and her surroundings at the same time.

Another flicker caught her attention, something rising from beneath the suspended walkway on her left, away from the wall.

Okay, this might be getting a little hot. Her own heart was pulsing a thump thump rhythm in her ears in the quiet of the concourse.

A bulbous tendril slowly surged onto the walkway. She fired a quick laser burst into it. The exploring blob retreated.

She backed off, away from the fire and away from the trail of mold. She moved further along the unexplored walkway. Her heels clicked; her finger tapped the trigger guard. She could feel time in the tight grip of her teeth.

Then another off-color flicker drew her attention behind her. A pink-orange mound the size of an ottoman was coming full speed, right for her, center of the walkway.

She waited. A good angle would make this easy. She watched it flex and flow at the edges, like a hypersonic farm slug.

When it was nearly close enough to reach out and touch, her phaser was pointed more down than out. She let loose with a heavy trigger finger. One pulse... four pulses. The force pushed the blob sideways until it came to rest against a handrail support.

The phaser had her ears ringing, and had shredded the blob. The sharp stench of caustic ichor scratched her throat and eyes in a familiar way.

She didn't even have to light this one herself. The dying fire of the last kill found new blood and sputtered to renewed life.

She was done here. She'd tell the maintenance office about the leak and they'd come down here with flamethrowers and laser bots and scorch the place.

Then they'd fix the leak. Or, they'd ignore her completely, because they were toothless like that.

She left the blazing hot nucleus behind without a second thought. Ten minutes ago she'd been there for money, now her goal was survival. She walked back the way she'd come. The skin of her neck prickled, urging her to a run, but she kept putting one foot in front of the other. She kept alert, refusing to focus only on her destination. Running just got you dead.

Halfway back to the ominous mold trail, she glimpsed another flicker. A good 20 feet in front of her some little texture shift had caught her eye. The blob wasn't moving, though—she couldn't tell its size or even where it was.

The damn blobs were flocking to this place like spacers to free whiskey.

She paused, watching, hoping for a little more information, but nothing happened. It didn't move.

Her neck prickled harder. Her metaphorical hackles were straight up.

Sometimes a blob froze like that. Usually she'd laser it, just to get an idea of what she was dealing with. But every instinct she had was screaming at her to get the fuck out.

She'd head for the other wall, then. Finish the path she hadn't yet tread. She turned around, yet again, and stretched her neck.

Anelace made it four steps, and then a sky of hazy gel slowly started falling toward her.

She dove into a run and she didn't look back, because hell, that thing was big. She had an impression of largeness, a sheet of a blob, but she couldn't stop to study it. She just moved, body straining for speed, and wondered why she wasn't dead. Running, really running, took concentration.

She swallowed a giddy laugh.

A pulsing tendril of palest green flowed from the walkway above her, swinging in air.

The same blob? A new one? Was she surrounded by death?

She fired her laser into goo, and the tendril whipped away. But a second tendril, the same pale green, pushed over the edge of the walkway a few feet in front of her.

She ducked right, back peddling. But behind her the blob was flowing down, stretched thin between the two walkways.

It was huge, it was in front of her and behind her both, and it could move fast. Yet she realized it wasn't even hurrying. It was flowing, it was advancing, but it hadn't struck. Yet.

She ducked around the tendril and dived for the edge of the walkway. She sprung forward to somersault over the rail. The rail was soot darkened and twisted, glowing brightly with heat from the recent blob bonfire underneath it. And it was too late to reverse her neat flip.

She landed on the shop roof below and rolled in a sloppily a controlled motion.

It didn't hurt, not yet... And then it hurt. Her lower abdomen radiated a hot agony, the kind she wanted to clutch, but knew she shouldn't. It wasn't the nerve-killing pain of a blob burn, but horrible pain was horrible pain. She throttled back a scream. Screaming could get addictive.

Then she scrambled for her feet, hobbling along, one arm protectively hovering near her stomach, daring to glance back.

The pale green blob was a pretty color, like an algae filled pool or exotic cocktail. It roiled down the face of the two levels, neatly piling itself on the rooftop behind her.

For the first time today, she wasn't just scared, she was shaken. Where in the blazing hells had that thing found enough to eat to reach that size?

Anelace pulled an incendiary grenade off her belt, one of two, expensive as fuck and of questionable legality. She flipped the pin and threw it behind her, an overhand pitch right into the seething mass. The blob closed around the grenade, trying to eat the damned thing.

A muffled roar sounded, an explosion wrapped in thick wool. She felt the concussion in her feet, up her legs and torso, clicking her teeth. The goo chasing her shuddered.

But damage to the blob seemed minimal; no fire started, no pieces fell off.

She ran faster, legs pumping, feet quick. Dust was a gritty texture under the thick soles of her work boots, a suffocating layer in her lungs. She jumped to the next roof and glanced back. Inexorable, the blob was still chasing.

It hesitated at the two-foot gap between roofs. At that blob's size, two feet wasn't a problem, but it still paused.

A wide, thick tendril bridged the distance, a column of blob as tall as she was and nearly as thick.

She took a shooter's stance, setting her laser to eleven of ten and firing. Vaporized gel puffed from a hole the size of a netball—a hole big enough to kill a person. But this wasn't a person.

The rest of the blob shifted around, pulling the injured bit into itself. No ichor flowed. She hadn't pierced its hide.

And now the laser's battery was empty. Frustration was her greedy, focus-stealing companion. Fuck!

Then it was tendrils everywhere. The barely-dented blob surged onto her roof, no more messing around.

She ran. The whistle of her own breathing sounded loud even in the open space.

So far the encounter had been all move, no stare, but she was getting an idea of size. The blob was the size of a room—the living area in her quarters, perhaps. She hadn't known they got this big. No one did.

The roofs she ran on formed a rough circle around a thick center column. The smaller shops she'd started with were further in, another ring four feet about this one. On her current level, each rooftop ended with a short lip. She jumped to the next roof, and whipped around.

The blob was still close, right behind her at the gap, with a column of questing tendril sticking straight into the air. It was perfectly situated for her to take a shot, but her laser was dead and the phaser would do zilch to something this big.

She pulled two homemade mines and a sizzler from a little pocket, dropping them behind her. And ran.

The mines were small, the size of a local half-credit, but had a good concussive bang. Usually, that concussion just flung the blob around, which they weren't too impressed by. But on a blob this big, there would be no flinging. Maybe that force would be channeled to break the blob's hide.

The sizzler was her own invention—a long strip of magnesium alloy attached to a temperature fuse.

The next time she turned, sucking in air, she watched the blob, watched the mines. It rolled over them, and a count later the first went off. The blob jumped, fluttering oddly where it absorbed the impact.

The second went off. Another jump.

She ran further, and now, finally, she could smell leaking ichor, and it was overpowering. Her eyes streamed tears.

And the blob was slowing. It had rotated its weak spots up, exposing dark purple wounds to sight, and she could see the eye-searing brightness of a magnesium fire buried somewhere deep in goo.

But it kept coming. Blobs didn't give up. And neither did she, though a line on her stomach throbbed with the deep pain of real injury and her steps drug with exhaustion.

She unclipped the handheld flamethrower from her belt, juggling to assemble it while trotting. She hated the flamethrower even more than the laser, but this situation called for a flamethrower. Putting it together on the run was like threading a needle during a knife fight, even with all her practice.

There were many cons to the flamethrower: assembly, low range, back splatter, station damage. The weapon had one pro, though: fire. Fire everywhere.

She veered left, running to the front of the shop. Without letting herself think about the pain to come, she dropped off the edge and caught herself with her hands. She hung, face to wall, while her stomach muscles pulled and her vision swam. Her fingers spasmed in sympathy with her damaged torso. When her grip released, she wasn't sure if she'd let go on purpose.

She fell an easy distance, landing on her feet.

She rocked as her knees absorbed the impact. She backed up a few steps and raised her flamethrower to ready.

She wasn't running in a circle on the shop rooftops anymore. How quickly would the blob notice?

Pretty damn quickly. It roiled over the lip of the roof above her, and she could see an oily slick of blob blood across its hide. She could feel her finger shaking on the trigger of the flamethrower, a fine little tremble driven by adrenaline and exhaustion.

She gave another couple steps. If it touched her, wrapped her in a thick tentacle, folded over her, coated her skin, or even just sprayed down on her, she'd die.

She let it get closer. A lift-sized puddle of blob was off the roof, flowing down the wall.

She pressed the first trigger, letting loose a thin stream of pressurized napalm. Then she squeezed the second trigger, lighting a spark of fire.

The flamethrower itself was small, with a long wand-like barrel, but it was generous with the napalm. A stream of fuel bloomed into a three-foot long spray of flame, bathing her arm in painful heat.

The blob surged away, back up the wall, and she chased it with flame. She swung her weapon in a wide arc across the blob, searing its skin. But the fire did not take. She could smell her hair burning. Her lungs fluttered and withered in her chest, attacked by the awful fumes of blob and napalm and fire. A greenish-white smoke had formed. But the fire did not take.

She brought the flamethrower back across, another slow arc, raising her hands to follow the blob as it fled.

Then the fire found something, and it surged higher in the wake of her hand. She backed up, fast, gasping for usable air. She only made it a couple steps away before the fire found a path through thick goo.

A magnificent pillar of flame whooshed upward, a phoenix.

She fell on her ass and crabbed further away on hands and feet. One of her legs wasn't working right, though, refusing to follow simple direction from her brain. She willed it to push and it just flopped. She heard herself whimpering, and, like a revelation, she felt the pain wrapping her ankle.

The blob burned in a fire to rival a foundry. Flames danced along the second floor walkway, and spread across the shop front.

She must have touched a few drops of blob blood, or landed on a little one. It had gotten between her reinforced boot and carbon-augmented denim pants, eating right through her sock.

She scrabbled a vial of oil from her belt, dumping it on the wound. The oil would prevent the wound from going deeper until she could get ointment on it.

Of course, the Devil-whoring jellyfish oil also made it impossible to feel her toes.

She stood up anyway. She was battered and bent, exhausted and in agony. Her lungs felt abraded. Her eyes ached from too many tears and her nose ran. But she would stay vigilant until the fire died.

Anelace had been exterminating for half her life, torching the most dangerous pests on the station, and she was still alive. You didn't survive that if you couldn't ignore a little pain.

Anelace slowly limped into the bounty office, one foot dragging, half dead with exhaustion, smelling like a chemical cesspit. She had open wounds, burnt hair and swollen eyes. She was bent slightly, one arm hooked as a shield over her stomach, an upright fetal position.

Vince, the maintenance manager at the desk, barely glanced up—he'd seen worse.

The bounty office was a small room between the sector claim office and the homestead office, in the station government hall. It was in a far forward area; the lifts mostly worked, up here. The walls were blue plastic panels hung from the ceiling, the desk had a giant dent, and there were dust bunnies in every corner.

Vince was a salted pro with too much hair, too many wrinkles, and too few teeth. There was a burn scar on his neck and the hand clutching his pencil was a finger shy of a standard five.

She turned so he could see the two-foot nucleus strapped to her back.

His eyes opened wide and his wrinkled lips sagged a little. "You're shitting me. That's fake."

Anelace shrugged a cord off her shoulder, moving to set the brittle scorched sphere on his desk.

"Whore's balls, don't you dare. Put it on the floor."

She set it on the floor instead.

"There isn't even have a price category for that one. That thing was, what, the size of a lift?"

"Bigger. The nuclei ran small."

Vince gave her a disbelieving look; why, she didn't know. She never lied about the size of her kills.

"You should have just run for it. It's not worth it."

Anelace shrugged, just a little bit, but it pulled at her stomach. She grimaced.

Vince counted out her credits, local cash into her hand and universal credits into her bank account.

"So when you kill yourself pulling these stupid stunts, who gets your money?"

Anelace's amusement drained with a long exhale. Good air tasted wonderful, like being alive, but her lungs were still pretty unhappy with her.

No one. The last of her family died when she was seventeen. And she wouldn't have given her father a dime anyway.

"Just transfer the hell's damned money, Vince." She sounded like four kinds of bitch, but she didn't care. She wanted off her feet.

He grimaced, but stopped dogging her.

After a moment in silence, her satisfaction slowly returned. It was hard to bring her down on a good payday. If Meidani could fix the gnawing pain in her lower abdomen, at least enough to keep her walking, she'd be golden.

When Meidani had seen Anelace walk through the door of the No Name, she'd paused in place. Then she'd motioned for the back and set down her rag.

Now they were back in the little storeroom, a plastic sheet across the table and Meidani's hands sanitized.

"Well, your arm looks like it's healing well," Meidani said.

"I had a good doctor."

Meidani blushed faintly. She always seemed to find the simplest of compliments awkwardly outrageous, and Anelace never ran out of compliments. She liked the blushing.

"What did you hurt?"

"Well, there's a blob burn on my ankle, pretty bad."

"Okay." Meidani bent for her foot.

"And some burns on my wrists, normal burns."

Meidani reached for her hands, instead, turning them to inspect the angry splotch of red. Her gloves couldn't protect the skin above the band.

"Okay. And your limp?"

"Just jellyfish oil, nothing big."

Then Anelace hesitated. Most of the time Meidani was sweet as honey, but she could get a bit prickly about injuries—maybe because she felt Anelace got too many of them. Which, actually, was kind of fun, but only because she was saucy when riled. It wouldn't be fun if she fired Anelace as a patient.

"Oh, just spit it out."

Anelace raised an eyebrow at her.

"You always get that guilty look when you've got a bad one."

"I burnt my stomach. That wasn't a blob, I don't think."

She was damn sure it wasn't. She remembered well the metal railing, still hot from the minor bonfire of her last kill, and the exact moment she threw herself against it. That moment had been a rather painful one.

She tugged apart the hook clasps on her vest. Then she pulled a black cotton tank top out of her pants, refusing to wince when it scratched across seeping blisters. It hurt, though. It really hurt.

Meidani sucked air across her teeth. "Anelace, you idiot. This is bad. You need to go to the med office."

"I've had worse," she said stoically.

"And you went to the med office."

"And that's why I can't go back. I'm going to end up on a list."

One trip to the med office for burns was an accident, two was bad luck. After five accidents in two years, the company might get worried about ending up with a human decency violation for running a station overflowing with carnivorous amoeba. They started thinking about locking you up for your own protection.

Meidani's forehead was pinched with a worry line. Her lips were pursed tight.

"If this gets infected, you're going to the med office if I have to phaser you and drag you there myself," she said.

Yep, Meidani was furious. Somehow, the woman looked sweet even when scowling, which would probably piss her off further to hear.

"It won't get infected."

"Yeah? Why not?"

"You're fixing me up." Anelace blasted her best charming smile.

Meidani just got angrier. "You idiot."

Meidani made incoherent grumbly noises low in her throat while she broke out a different jar of ointment and a box of bandage pads.

"Come on, it doesn't look THAT bad."

And it really didn't. The burn was the size of two fingers, stretching just below her belly button. It was an unnatural red-purple color and painful, but the blisters were small. Ow.

Meidani's eyes flashed. "Just you wait until tomorrow. You idiot."

Anelace kept her mouth shut. She didn't want to be called an idiot again.

Her doctor was often annoyed with her when she was injured, but this was a bit more. Tweaking her now seemed like a bad idea.

Just because she found it cute when Meidani called her names didn't mean either of them would enjoy it if Meidani hit full-out rage.

Meidani reached for the top button of Anelace's jeans. Hesitated.

Anelace reached down to help, but Meidani snapped out of her distraction. She hooked her hand through the waistband, fingers brushing skin made sensitive by pain and a hint of fever, and unhooked the button.

Anelace was so damn beat, she didn't even feel pervy about Meidani unbuttoning her pants. The universe was constructed of small favors.

Meidani tugged the waistband a little lower and spread an ointment using a long sterile stick. While Meidani slathered, she talked. "You have to come back later today to get this off."

Anelace nodded.

Meidani grabbed her face, holding her chin with a firm hand and making intense eye contact.

"Hey, what..."

Meidani's hand felt so good on her face, soft and firm and warm. She wanted to turn her face into it like a cat. Her day was catching up with her and she just really wanted that touch.

"Listen to me. Listening? This isn't a blob burn. We have to change the dressing and you have to pay attention. This skin is going to die and it has to come off. If you do anything wrong or maybe if you everything right, it might get infected. I mean necrosis, Anelace, you idiot. You could die. Really die."

Meidani's eyes were dark enough to swallow Anelace's playful rejoinder. Meidani was dead serious, and worried, and upset.

The fun of an angry Meidani melted into the nagging feeling Anelace was an asshole.

"I promise. Exactly what you say."

"No sani. No showering at all."

"God as my witness. When people complain I stink, I'll say doctor's orders."

Meidani let go of her patient's face and dabbed a little more ointment. It felt soothing going on, and quickly started to numb the pain. She liked this ointment much better than the jellyfish stuff used on blob burns.

"Don't get me taken in for illegal medicine, either." Now she worked with calm efficiency. "And you need antibiotics. A full spread. You know where to get some, right?"

"Wait, what? It's a burn! Antibiotics are controlled."

Controlled meant expensive.

"What did I just say to you? Infection is bad."

"Meidani."

"The med office will give you antibiotics, for free. Just drop in. They'll give you the shot right there."

"And cite me for self-endangerment."

"And you are a danger, so that would be accurate, wouldn't it? But I guess you wouldn't want that, so you'll have to go buy antibiotics from Lara," Meidani said brightly.

Anelace scowled. Meidani knew damn well she didn't want to buy antibiotics, and her cheerfulness while suggesting it was just mocking.

"Not Lara. She doesn't like me."

Lara had caught Anelace cheating on her when they were both nineteen, before Anelace had figured out how bad she was at being tied down. Lara's hatred had petered out, and eventually she'd even accepted Anelace's apology, but that didn't mean she had forgiven. Anelace would be lucky to escape that deal with both her kidneys.

Now, Anelace wasn't much better at keeping women happy. But at least she didn't cheat.

Satisfied with a thick layer of ointment, Meidani stretched an even thicker layer of gauze across her abdomen. Her touch on Anelace's stomach was delicate and sure.

After the gauze came the tape—more tape than seemed necessary. A taut noise of pulling and tearing drowned the soft clang of gambling sin. Then the quiet whoosh of a thumb pressing tape followed. Her doctor ran her thumb along each strip, well clear of the edges of the wound, pressing it firmly.

Meidani took a deep, quiet breath, preparing herself to say something Anelace probably wouldn't like. Oh man. How mad was she?

Meidani closed her mouth, her thought unvoiced.

Then she took another deep breath, the edges of her teeth pearly behind her lips.

"I think you owe me," she said.

"Of course." Anelace reached for her pocket.

"No. I mean, like you said—for fun. You owe me a good time."

Meidani was talking to her hands. Her shyness was kicking in full force, which she hadn't done around just Anelace in weeks.

The kid?

"You should take me out for a date."

Anelace's entire world shifted, slowly, like a gravity drive out of alignment. Five minutes ago, Anelace had only seduced wild girls and her doctor friend was probably straight. Now?

"Okay. Of course. May I show you a good time, Meidani?" Anelace asked with teasing politeness.

Meidani laughed. "Yes. And you owe my fee, too."

And with that delighted laugh tickling her ears, Anelace forgot every down side to lusting after her doc.

THREE

A quaint white door retracted with a brisk swoosh, revealing Meidani on the other side. Her eyes were huge and her color bright. Her hair, long, black, and shiny, was gathered in a partial knot and a real primrose was pinned beside her face.

Her dress was lavender, tailored cotton hugging Meidani's curves intimately. The sleeves were gathered, the skirt full and past her knees. It was a long skirt, but it was anything but matronly.

She looked like something ethereal. Anelace's fingers twitched to free the flower, to run through the thick river of Meidani's hair. She would hand the flower back to her and kiss her lips, to taste if she was real.

"You just going to stare?" Brisco asked.

Anelace looked over at the towering lump of man flesh standing beside Meidani, a big smirk on his face.

Brisco, Meidani's half brother, took after his father. His skin was the pink of a fat baby and his shoulders wide, a surprising contrast to his sister. Meidani was petite and her skin a dark olive shade.

Anelace liked him well enough, but she gave him the 'don't mess with me' stare anyway. He smirked harder.

"Goodnight, Brisco." Meidani said.

She stepped through the door, and Anelace's thought stuttered on how close she stood. The whole week had been like that. It was as if Anelace finally had permission to perv on Meidani, and her imagination was going to make up for lost time.

"Wait." They both paused. "Exterminator, you'll walk her home?"

"Yes, of course."

Women didn't walk anywhere alone on the station, unless you counted Anelace. Anelace didn't.

"And have her home by twenty-two hundred."

"I don't think so. I'll be home when I'm home." Meidani hit the button for the manual door override. It slid shut in his face.

Anelace offered the crook of her elbow in a courtly gesture. Meidani's mouth twitched, but she took it. Together, they walked toward the promenade.

Meidani's family lived close in, in a nice, clean-smelling hall. You could tell the neighbors rarely got drunk and puked as they stumbled home.

Meidani's hand was warm against Anelace's skin, a pleasant heat that Anelace couldn't make herself ignore. It was distracting and comforting and awakening.

Was Meidani thinking the same thing? Was this tension two-sided for once? Anelace couldn't say, and it was a weird feeling after a lifetime of knowing where she stood with women.

Meidani noticed Anelace sneaking looks at her face, and her mouth formed a secretive little smile. An edible looking smile.

Pressing Meidani to the wall for a messy, gasping, desperate kiss before the date even started would probably be rude.

Anelace wrapped her hand around Meidani's hand where it hooked Anelace's arm.

Meidani broke the quiet. "I've been wanting to get my own place."

She could do that. Moving out wasn't hard—there were hundreds of unoccupied living quarters. But there were dangers to living on your own.

"Yeah? What did your family think of that?"

"Hellfire and brimstone. Gravity failing and unregulated nuclear fission. Cats and dogs living together."

"You had to see that coming."

"I'm still going to do it. Someday."

Anelace reigned in an urge to agree with Meidani's family. Seduction step one: don't mother a gal.

Life off the family homestead could be hard. Blobs encroached, important systems failed, miners rampaged and stationers were no better. Anelace slept with a phaser on her nightstand and a knife under her pillow. She didn't like to imagine Meidani living that way, but Meidani wouldn't take kindly to Anelace voicing her protective urges. Meidani already got a lot of that from her family, from Lupe's family, from her mother's husband Big Zed and from every damn person who'd worked for him in thirty years as Master of the Port.

"I'll get you an illegal shotgun for your housewarming gift."

"Thanks," Meidani coated the word in delicious sarcasm, but her mouth quirked in a little smile.

They went rockward—toward what remained of the asteroid the station was built to engulf—and out toward a ramping hall. They avoided the lifts. Only a few people had died on stuck lifts, but why tempt fate?

They walked down sloped, switchback halls lined by sterile white plastic. There were a few holes where limbs had gone through cheap, brittle paneling, but it was clean and the blobs didn't eat this stuff. Distantly she heard someone talking, but they didn't come near.

And then the smell changed—a hint of dust, a sheen of mildew and the strong odor of sour tobacco.

They stepped through a wide wooden arch into the second story of the promenade, across from the spaceport entrance. Anelace had an eerie moment of déjà vu. The half-healed skin of her stomach twitched in painful memory.

The spaceport concourse was built from the same plan as the lower section deathtrap maintenance was still ignoring. A scattered-block pattern built into a pile of white stucco shops, though it was so dim you could barely see them. Walkways swooped through the gloom, and the ceiling soared high overhead. That was the end to similarities.

The outer walls and walks were paneled in mottled wood, styled after the station's namesake. The bulkhead eight stories up was dark, the light-sky long dead. On each level, bunches of paper lanterns hung from strings, circles and squares and fishes, fighting the dimness with pools of light.

It was still early, but it was loud. People yelling, music blasting on four levels. Barkers and buskers and scantily clad hostesses were setting up outside doorways. And on every level, there were people walking between shops in twos or fives, the closest thing to a crowd you could find on Rosewood.

Meidani glanced over at her curiously. Anelace didn't say a word, just led onward.

She'd gone over their options all morning. Her preferred date spot was the No Name, but Meidani worked there. You didn't take a woman back to the bar she earned her paycheck in.

Other options were the upper floor bars, mixed amongst the brothels, rough places with crude entertainments. There was the Midnight Club, with strobing lights to hide the ratty leather. There were gambling halls and dancing halls and massage parlors. It all depended on your definition of fun.

Anelace led Meidani toward the center shops, kitten-heeled white sandals and black dress boots both clicking on the rough wood floor.

The way this usually went, Anelace would impress a woman with champagne imported from off-station at a 600% markup, then they'd switch to sex. The sex would continue until Anelace forgot to drop by one too many times. Then came more champagne.

She couldn't imagine Meidani in any part of that scenario.

They crossed to the little shop, second floor, inner stack, and Anelace held open an old-fashioned hinged door, painted blue and dwarfed by the pitted wood of the storefront around it. Meidani stopped.

"Really?"

"I hear the cream is real."

"My grandmother comes here."

"If we're lucky, not tonight."

Meidani's smile grew, a laugh building behind glossy lips.

"I was expecting tequila shots and table dancing."

"You can dance on a table. I doubt anyone would mind."

Meidani shook her head and swept into Mrs. Blywigg's tea shop. The dress did amazing, hugging, swishing things to her legs. And her ass.

The shop was a comfortable mix of frilly and worn. Lacy white curtains covered the only window to the concourse, and the walls had thick floral wallpaper. The tables were mismatched and their centerpieces were bright fake flowers.

Ms. Blywigg herself greeted them with a long history of high tea and her shop. First wave settlers, from European Earth, had brought it into space as a novelty on the long-haul ships, but rarely practiced the custom. Second wave settlers, a joint venture between the Chinese and Indian nations, had followed. When the two groups started meeting each other again in the reaches of space, the high tea had come to symbolize peaceful negotiation and communication and a memory of shared tradition. Also, cookies.

Meidani listened raptly while they were seated, and Mrs. Blywigg authoritatively chose a tea for them then headed for the back.

"You come here often?" Meidani asked.

"No, my first time. You? With your grandmother?"

"My first time too."

They perused tiny paper menus decorated with florid plant illustrations. It was quiet, but comfortable quiet. They'd spent just enough time together over the last six months to find an easiness that strangers didn't have. Small talk between them was rare. Meidani could be painfully quiet, known to go hours at a time without speaking. Anelace talked more, but couldn't care less about the things that fueled a meaningless conversation.

Meidani absently pushed some of her hair behind her ear. For the third time in five minutes.

And perhaps Anelace was feeling just a bit nervous. Meidani wanted to have a little fun, and Anelace would very much enjoy giving it to her. But what were the nicer woman's limits? Too much might send her fleeing in horror. Too little was an opportunity squandered. She wanted to get this right. That little hesitation when Meidani had asked for it was important. And sexy. And a lot of pressure.

Mrs. Blywigg spoke beside them and Anelace startled in her chair. Meidani smiled the entire time they ordered.

Their first round of tiny little sandwiches arrived, and they spoke briefly about Anelace's wound (doing well) and the feral dogs below the long-term food pods (Anelace would be careful). She loved it when Meidani really got into a topic, babbling her head off despite her often shy demeanor. And she knew to pay attention—she'd seen too many assholes try to talk right over a woman for being quieter or less pushy than they were.

After the small talk, they fell into a more comfortable silence. It gave Anelace plenty of time to form a new religion worshipping that simple lavender dress, wrapping in front to hug Meidani's breasts. The fabric bisected just right, taut over firm swells. Her cleavage wasn't deep, it didn't meet, but it was just so very pleasant.

"Why do you let me be quiet?"

Anelace froze, pretty sure she'd just be caught staring at Meidani's boobs, a delicate china cup halfway to her mouth.

"I was just wondering," Meidani said.

Anelace had to parse what she'd meant. She figured it out, after an awkward pause. "You seem to want that. Sometimes, you don't like to talk."

"Yes, but everyone makes me talk anyway. They ask questions, 'draw me out', tell me I'm too quiet. No one just lets me be."

"But do you want to talk? Do you like being drawn out?"

"No. It's annoying."

"Then I don't do that."

Meidani smiled. She liked that answer.

A warm flush lingered in Anelace's body, a gentle promise to her libido that hey, yeah, maybe those sweet smiles could be turned into gasps.

They finished their tea slowly, lingering together over cookies.

Meidani's smile kept returning; she was enjoying herself. Anelace was pleasantly relieved to realize they did have chemistry, no matter how nice Meidani was or how rough her own edges were.

"We could go somewhere you like," Meidani suggested, setting aside her cup.

"I like it here."

"You like it, but not that much. You wouldn't come here on your own. Where would you go, if it was just you?"

"The No Name."

"Oh no, not there."

Anelace raised an eyebrow.

"Don't do that. It makes me jealous. Mine doesn't do that."

Her eyebrow? Anelace raised it again, showing off.

Meidani raised both eyebrows back at her with a little frown of concentration, obviously trying for just one. It made her look surprised by life.

Anelace laughed, and laughed more at Meidani's pathetic attempt to look grumpy.

"But really. Where's the last place you went that wasn't the No Name?" Meidani asked.

Mostly, Anelace stayed home. She almost suggested that—going home; it would be fun. It would be a naked Meidani, moaning and writhing. Very fun for both of them.

It might be too early to hope for that. She didn't know how well Meidani wanted to know a lover. She knew Meidani had dated a couple girls as a teen, but she didn't know where sex figured into that.

But she knew Meidani was smiling. She knew her own body felt oversensitive, warm with promise. She knew they had chemistry, and this was going... somewhere. A tingle of anticipation walked up her spine.

Unless she messed it up.

What were they talking about? Anelace blinked. Meidani was looking at her expectantly, and her smile grew. Something about the expression on Anelace's face gave Meidani that mischievous smile.

"The Olive Branch. I had a big payday off that bounty last week. I celebrate at the Olive Branch whenever that happens."

Meidani frowned.

"It's a good place to talk about weapons."

The Olive Branch drew off-station visitors, but not miners. The crowd was about half mercenary and security, and half crew from the sort of small, scruffy ships that weren't above the occasional act of piracy. The saloon was known amongst stationers for its deadly brawls, on a station where brawls were commonplace.

"Locals don't know much about extermination, even the exterminators. The Olive Branch has people who use the same gear I do, and some have space vermin to deal with. And the men don't hit on you like the chicken-fucking miners."

"We could go to The Olive Branch," Meidani said.

Anelace started to raise an eyebrow again. Meidani put her hand on Anelace's face, hiding the offending feature. They both dissolved into laughter, though neither were usually gigglers.

"Or we could have more of these cookies. They're amazing," Anelace said.

"Shortbread? I can make shortbread."

"Oh, really?" Anelace asked in her best insinuating voice, making Meidani laugh again.

She loved watching Meidani laugh. Her face changed. Her whole body changed. She got loose and happy and it was sexy as hell.

Then Meidani changed the subject.

"I asked about you, you know. About dating you."

Anelace was surprised to hear it. Then again, she was getting used to being surprised by this woman.

"Who did you ask?"

Meidani shrugged. "Oh, everybody."

"I haven't dated quite everybody."

Meidani didn't dignify her smart-assery with a response.

Unrepentant, Anelace grinned. She could tease Meidani for hours. All night. Gasping and...

Right. Mind back on conversation.

"What did everybody say?"

"They said you're bad news. You're a troublemaker, and a hellcat, and you're fast, and you never call later," she recounted, perfectly serious. But her smile was still there, still secretive.

"Oh really?"

It was accurate, but Anelace hadn't realized it was common knowledge. Meidani might want better than that. Then again, that's who Anelace had been since she was born, more or less. She didn't apologize for it.

"Why did you come out with me then?"

Meidani shrugged the question away, but answered. "I'm hoping it's true."

Anelace laughed. "That I'm a troublemaker?"

"Yes." Meidani's face turned serious. Her eyes were sparking with emotion. The look intimidated and thrilled Anelace at the same time.

"And that you're fast. You better be planning to take me home, after I got all dressed up for you," she finished.

Anelace began to choke on absolutely nothing.

They shared a dozen laughs on the way back to Anelace's quarters. Once there, through her shabby front door, Anelace stopped.

Meidani's smile was wide, transforming her elegance into something artless. Her flower had drooped and a wisp of hair lay across her face, caught in her eyelashes. Her eyes were bright with humor.

In contrast, the entryway was utilitarian. A narrow two-step transition through a bulkhead, it wasn't meant for lingering. The light was too bright, the wall unsheathed metal, the floor a scuffed plastic tile. It framed Meidani's perfection like she was art.

Anelace held eye contact and leaned in. She swept her mouth across Meidani's in a warm, dry touch—the kiss was so simple, but Anelace felt it like a tingling at her mouth, a feeling of pleasure that spread down her throat, through her body.

Meidani gasped softly. When she exhaled, Anelace felt the breath as a fan on her cheek. Anelace shuddered and closed her own eyes.

Overeager excitement welled in Anelace, and a weird bubbling happiness. They had a spark between them—a spark like a plasma welder. And Meidani had felt it too.

Anelace had been worried, just a little bit. Nice girls were a strange species she had rarely met—who could say what they liked?

Meidani moved for another kiss, and Anelace met her. She slid the tiniest tip of her tongue over Meidani's lips, tracing delicate contour. Meidani's mouth immediately parted, inviting her deeper.

Anelace teased instead, nibbling softly at Meidani's bottom lip.

Tonight, Meidani was out to have fun. She was trying new things, feeling new thrills, experimenting like a schoolgirl. Anelace wanted to be a good experiment. She wanted to be perfect for her. She didn't know why it was so important. But it was. Nervousness tightened the air in her throat.

She quashed it down. Innocent fun wasn't her style, but neither was performance anxiety.

The next kiss, Anelace slid her tongue into Meidani's mouth, licking playfully. They liked that, both of them, and took a while to explore. With each brush of their lips, Anelace took a little more, and Meidani's breathing got a little deeper.

"You taste sweet," Meidani murmured.

Anelace tasted Meidani's shoulder, licking the small bump of her clavicle near lavender neckline. "So do you."

Meidani rolled her eyes. "I meant sweet from the tea."

"Tea? Hrmmm... Let me taste again."

Anelace brushed her lips across Meidani's shoulder, and Meidani's body shook with laughter. Her skin was soft, free of scars Anelace nuzzled the hollow of her neck and trailed her lips slowly up to her earlobe. She kissed and nibbled and kissed again, exploring Meidani's throat and shoulders.

The scent of Meidani filled her nostrils—a little makeup, a little shampoo, something delicately human that had no words. Plus vanilla. Always vanilla. She must use it as a perfume. Anticipation was a warm current in Anelace's body, building, soon to turn to wild electricity. She liked this. She liked slow and exploring and loose.

She would be slow if it killed her.

She could feel every breath Meidani took with her lips, a subtle vibration. She tasted every uncertainty, every hitched breath. And when Meidani sighed, Anelace felt it under her touch.

Anelace trailed her mouth across the satiny cloth of Meidani's dress, over the tense swell of Meidani's breast. Anelace lifted her hand to gently cup sensitive flesh, and with the next movement of her face she brushed her lips across Meidani's perked nipple. The thumb of her other hand emulated the soft caress of her lips.

Meidani let out a long quivering breath, and Anelace shuddered in response. She glanced up.

The doc's eyes were closed and her eyelashes were long and dark, laying gently against the warm honey-tint of her skin. Her bottom lip was caught between her teeth and the muscles of her throat tight with arousal. She was so beautiful.

Lust kicked Anelace hard. Her hand twitched to grab and hold. Like a brat after candy, she wanted more, now, all. Her need wasn't playful, and this didn't feel like just fun.

Anelace kissed Meidani again, and this time it wasn't sweet. She stroked Meidani's tongue with her own, demanding pleasure for both of them. While their tongues tangled, she stepped close, pressing Meidani into the wall.

Meidani hooked her hand over Anelace's belt, pulling her closer. Pulling at Anelace's jeans. Lust was a pulse through Anelace's body, a rogue desire to rub against her date like an oversexed teen boy.

But she didn't. Slow, damnit.

Anelace's hands massaged Meidani's breasts, thumbs tracing an insistent pattern. Soft fabric glided over silky skin.

Meidani's breath was gasping, her face flushed with red. She made a noise, a little noise in the back of her throat.

Anelace ended the kiss. She wanted to hear the woman against her moan. She wanted to hear quiet Meidani's voice fill the room with gasps and words and whimpers of pleasure. She caressed lower, her hand gliding down Meidani's stomach.

"Can I go lower?" Anelace whispered.

Meidani's mouth gapped open. Her fingers rose to touch her lips. A little laugh escaped her mouth, frail and nervous.

Anelace faltered. Her hand slowed, moving to rest on Meidani's hip.

She knew she could be intense in bed, and she knew that made some women uncomfortable. She needed to restrain that with Meidani, or she'd ruin the night. Meidani would get self-conscious, and then she wouldn't be having fun. Meidani was going to have fun, or Anelace would die trying.

"Someone's gone down on you before, right? One of those kids you date?"

"I don't date kids," Meidani pointed warningly at Anelace.

Anelace playfully bit her finger.

"Did you like it?"

"No..."

Right. Bad idea.

"But we could try again."

Anelace peered at Meidani's face, studying, undecided. Was she humoring her? Would she enjoy the attempt?

After a moment, Meidani crossed her eyes back at her. Then she awkward laughed.

Anelace slid to her knees, making the woman laugh again. She nuzzled her cheek into Meidani's skirt, enjoying its cool crispness. Then she raised it with her hands, brushing her cheek across the soft skin of Meidani's thigh.

Her underwear was lavender, a silky match to her dress. Wearing matching underwear was lady-like and prim, and Anelace rubbing her face across those panties was so fucking hot she squirmed while she did it. Hot desire was a pool of sensation in her core.

Slowly, Meidani relaxed under her caress. Anelace hooked her fingers in the panties, pulling them down Meidani's legs.

"Should we move to your bed?" Meidani asked softly.

Anelace paused. "Now? That's like fifteen steps away. Too far."

"Oh, it is. Wow, your place is pretty big." Her voice changed to interested distraction.

Anelace kissed Meidani gently, the shape of her folds impressed on Anelace's lips. She licked, a little taste, then a wider swipe of her tongue. Meidani was sweet and wet—but Anelace wanted her wetter. She wanted her messy and moaning. Bridled anticipation shot through Anelace, phantom pleasure dancing across nerve endings. She closed her eyes against the imagined image.

"And you've decorated. I like your pictures. Do they change?" Meidani's voice caught only a little right at the end.

Was Meidani really trying to trade small talk with a face buried in her pussy?

Anelace laughed.

"Relax. Hold this," Anelace pressed an edge of Meidani's dress into her hands. "Lean back. Tell me what you like. Tell me what you don't."

Meidani shifted, settling her weight against the wall.

"I like your pictures."

Anelace gently nuzzled her clit, shutting Meidani right up. Then she licked again. She explored with her tongue, tracing sparse pubic hair.

Her tongue felt rough, but only because Meidani's intimate folds were silky soft. She sucked gently and stroked across her clit, promising then delivering. And when she found a motion that made Meidani sigh, she did it again.

Meidani didn't speak a word, but her arousal was obvious. Her stance had loosened and wetness gleamed between her thighs. Her clit was sensitive, a prominent nub.

Meidani's hands caught in Anelace's hair, began to massage her scalp. Fingers, the tips of hard fingernails, traced lines of pleasure across her head. What could have been a relaxer bloomed through her lust-drenched body. Ecstasy came in little chasers down her spine, straight to her cunt. She clenched her thighs and moaned against Meidani's body, which sparked an answered moan.

Anelace pressed a stiff tongue into Meidani's entrance. Meidani gasped and pressed her hips forward. "That," she croaked with a malfunctioning voice.

So Anelace pressed her thumb into Meidani's core. It was the kind of teasing penetration that could drive a woman crazy. Meidani pumped her hips against the digit in reflexive little motions. Anelace swirled her tongue, driving the movements faster.

Meidani's breath was coming thicker now, with desperate noises. Her hand tangled in Anelace's hair, a little too tight. Meidani had become demanding.

Anelace's body was throbbing in time to Meidani's hips. The smell, the taste of the other woman was imprinted on her brain like a firebrand in the dark. The moment was floating in a brain-bending wash of sexy.

Anelace gently drew Meidani's hooded clit between her lips. She sucked and stroked with her tongue, petting the nub.

Meidani's back arched and she rose up on her tiptoes. The moan pushing from her throat sounded vicious. Her orgasming body shuddered in Anelace's hands and Anelace's hands clenched around her thighs

Meidani's body slowly gentled. After another long second, she laughed. Anelace sat back on her heels.

Meidani needed a moment, and she wasn't the only one. Anelace's body had been swept along for the ride—the arousal, the pleasure, the immense tension—with no end in sight. She stood slowly, sensitive body objecting to the lack of attention.

"My legs are wobbly. Now the bed?" Meidani said.

Anelace helped Meidani rearrange her dress.

"So, was it fun?" Anelace asked.

Meidani gave up on the twisted dress, pulling it off over her head. She ignored the question, walking through the bedroom door wearing just white heeled sandals. Her thighs were strong, her ass full and rounded. Her waist stretched high up her torso, creating a perfect W shape. Anelace stared as she followed.

Her sleeping area was standard station quarters fare. A bed just big enough for two stretched between three walls, with a small walking area near the entrance archway. It was open to the outer room, which was good, because it was tiny.

Meidani sat on the bed to remove her shoes, and looked back at Anelace with a sharp gleam in her eyes. "Take off your clothes."

The blood in Anelace's body surged in answer. Was it possible to be so turned on you fainted?

Anelace obeyed. She shed boots and shirt, jeans and socks while Meidani watched. Her face held rapt attention. She was a porn watcher, a smut reader, a gambler in front of a slot machine.

That look devoured Anelace. Meidani didn't act like someone dabbling in the wild side. The sweet little doc seemed to understand wild—debauchery was at her beck and call.

Anelace remembered trying to fix her up with a good boy type, and realized she was an idiot.

Anelace joined the siren on the bed.

Meidani was waiting with a ready touch. She ran her fingers down Anelace's body, touching and shaping and staring with her hands. Anelace couldn't decide if she was indulging Meidani's sensual fascination, or basking in it.

Meidani tasted the curve of Anelace's shoulder, leaving sparks in her lips' wake. She ran a hand over

Anelace's hip, a touch of comfort and fire. She dropped her hot, wet mouth to Anelace's nipple, and Anelace could feel that warmth through to her core. Sensation was a spear of tingly need that had her squeezing her thighs together tight.

Meidani was a mussed siren now. Her lips were puffy and swollen. Her hair was falling loose and a faint mottled flush stained her chest and cheeks.

Anelace closed her eyes and gasped on thick tension. She pressed her own hand between her legs. She was wet. Her body was too hot. Her legs were thrown wide, one knee hooked over the edge of the bed. She circled a heavy finger against her clit, and pleasure was like an assault. Her head fell back and she made a noise that was half sob.

Meidani's hand closed over hers. "Let me. It's my turn."

Then she took Anelace's lips in a dominating kiss. Anelace bucked in the other woman's hands.

Meidani's fingers took over against her clit. She stroked faster, pushing her higher. Sparks detonated down her spine. Her pulse was a rising wave, flooding her body, taking over her mind. The higher she drifted, the harder her body throbbed—empty, needy, waiting. Meidani's weight against her side was comforting, and her fingers were punishing ecstasy.

Anelace started to panic. This didn't feel like just fun. This felt amazing, engulfing. It felt like a reckless leap over a gaping chasm, with her own fear waiting at the bottom to eat her alive.

But she wanted this. Anelace opened her eyes. Fun got old. Casual was hard.

Anelace gazed up into wide eyes, dark with intent. Meidani watched back, biting her own lip. Anelace's lip twinged in sympathy, or jealousy.

And that nimble hand was answering Anelace's confused gasps for more.

Meidani slid two fingers into Anelace's cunt, pressing easily into wetness. Anelace grabbed her wrist, a twitchy attempt to hold her hand hostage. Meidani let her. And then she kissed her again.

"Thank you," Anelace gasped. "Right like..."

Anelace pumped her hips, pumped Meidani's hand. She fucked herself, too wound up to cede control. That it was Meidani's fingers in her felt like a miracle.

"Come, Anelace. You want to," Meidani whispered.

"I need to," she gasped.

"You're so beautiful," Meidani mused, her words a caress of air on Anelace's neck.

Anelace strained to hear her, strained for release.

"I'm going to fuck you. Do you have a dildo? I'm going to get a toy and fuck you so hard," Meidani whispered.

Anelace's orgasm smacked her like a phaser blast. Her body bowed, her toes curled. Pleasure broke a dam in her body, and then it pumped through her with each careful stroke of Meidani's hand.

Then Anelace just tried to breathe.

Those dirty words had about killed her.

They both stilled, sinking into the bed, staring at each other.

"Fuck," Anelace said.

"Yes," Meidani agreed. Then they both chuckled.

They were still on laughter, the way sex had begun. But Anelace suspected something fundamental had changed. And she doubted they were done for the night.

FOUR

Anelace leaned against a wall, one brown and turquoise boot kicked over the other and her hat low on her forehead. Her hands were tucked into her pockets, her face neutral.

At the other end of the wide hall, a pair of huge doors marked the entrance to the New Covenant church. They were traditional hinged wood, painted three shades of green.

She waited for Meidani to come out. She had taken over as Meidani's escort, replacing her brothers on Sunday afternoon errands this week. And the longer she waited, the more insistent her craving for the other woman grew.

Fun had gotten a bit tangled over the last week, a right mess deep in Anelace's subconscious. They were just having a good time, right? She was Meidani's illicit thrill? Illicit thrills didn't run errands. Errands were usually a precursor to a woman getting serious and Anelace bailing out. And no woman suggested errands in the first week.

Except this time, Anelace had.

Apparently she was fast in more ways than one.

The heavy doors swung open, signaling the end of services. Anelace increased the nonchalance in her slouch. She wasn't a churchgoer. She risked a lecture from some biddy just by being there, but she wasn't afraid, and she was going to prove it by slouching.

The first few stationers trickled out, dressed in their Sunday best—white dresses, brown cotton trousers, prim little hats, well-blacked boots. Then the trickle swelled to a rush of ambling folk exchanging pleasantries and polite nods.

A few shot her second looks. One woman sniffed at her presence, or maybe her battered hat. Like blobs never got in the church.

Busybodies swiveled their necks in circles, making note of who was in the crowd, who wasn't, and who talked to whom.

Anelace would make a poor busybody. She recognized Lupe, the owner of the No Name, and the morning clerk from the company store. A couple of the whores from the upstairs brothels were there, each dressed in his Sunday suit, and the bouncer from the downstairs gambling hall preferred by grandmas and drunks.

She also recognized Mirna Steppen, holding the hand of a six-year old angel named Trish with blue bows in her curly blonde hair. The girl's other hand hung at her side, a twisted mess of flesh, barely useful enough to escape amputation.

Anelace's chest constricted. Neither Mirna nor Trish blamed Anelace for that injury, but that had never stopped Anelace from blaming herself. The month a toddling Trish had picked up a fun-looking little blob on the Section E6 playground, Anelace hadn't been around much. There'd been emergencies and pretty girls to buy whiskey for, and she'd had a flu for a little while there.

Keeping inhabited halls blob-free was supposed to be maintenance's job, but that was the thing about maintenance—in the end, they were company boys. And to hear the company tell it, playgrounds weren't essential upkeep.

Right. Little girls' hands weren't essential.

"Looking for me?" Meidani's sweet voice spoke softly from beside her.

"Yes. How'd I miss you?"

"I don't know. You were scowling something fierce, though."

Meidani was wearing a wide rattan hat, white, with a big blue flower covering half her head.

"You hid behind your hat." Anelace tweaked the brim with a flick of her fingers.

Meidani smacked her hand away, but she smiled. Teasing Meidani was one way to fix a dour mood, right quick.

"Can we get out of here?"

Meidani nodded gravely. Anelace stood, ignoring the intense urge to scratch her healing wound when the skin pulled tight. Instead, she offered her arm, and Meidani took the elbow in her hands.

Meidani wasn't always like this—traditional and girly and formal—but when she was, she took it seriously. Maybe it was the influence of her Sunday hat. It was adorable.

They walked slowly with the crowd, down the wide hall, past a set of green bulkheads. The New Covenant church was the focal point of stationer culture. The church had pride of place at the edge of the residential area, near the promenade concourse, and symbolic green marked the halls to and from.

A man Anelace recognized, but didn't know, tipped his hat at the both of them. "Ma'am, ma'am."

Meidani smiled at him and nodded a Sunday sort of hello. Anelace tugged her hat brim, neighborly-like, and they kept walking.

In the promenade, bunches of faded fake flowers hung from every third post. They were blue and white daisies, dusty and quaint. That was the only Sunday finery, though—the rest was the usual dusty wood floors, dim lighting and air tainted by tobacco smoke.

On the bottom floor, as they passed, a grand fountain shot water in a wide arc onto faded blue tile. The ambitious women of the station formed a cluster nearby. For those women, their Sunday best showed a little cleavage and ended above the knee. More women were joining them, coming from church. The miners, their chosen prey, were still abed.

Every woman on the station hoped to find her prince, the crude uneducated miner that could score a berth out of here on one of the company ships for their new bride. Except Anelace. Or Meidani. Or anyone with half an ounce of sense.

Anelace glanced over at her companion. Meidani's big white hat shielded her face from view.

At least the miners knew where they stood. Those women were harder mercenaries than even Anelace. Meidani, however, played her hand close.

Meidani glanced back at her. "The company store, first."

Anelace nodded and led them that way.

"So how has it been? The blobs?"

"Not too bad. A bit slow, even. Maintenance cleaned out a big mess in an old cafeteria and sealed that off. Also, one of the farms."

Anelace had been back to the abandoned concourse, whittling at the edges of that population, but she couldn't do more with that water leak still there.

Meidani nodded, a secretive little smile playing across her lips and Anelace's entire body warmed. What would that smile taste like? Would it feel as good against her lips as it looked on Meidani's face?

"You're in a good mood," Anelace said.

"I am." She tightened her grip on Anelace's elbow, and they ducked through the door of the Kao-Petersen General Mercantile.

The company store was staples and hardware, sold at a discount to company families like Meidani's. Everyone else paid their neighbors a slight markup just to get essentials.

"Do you need anything?" Meidani murmured.

"I'm good."

With Anelace in tow, Meidani browsed, filling a handheld basket. It was a casual shopping trip, just two women enjoying time together while taking care of some errands. She'd never done this before.

Oh, she'd dated, of course. She'd taken women dancing, she'd bought them gifts, she'd spent a lot of time in bed. Casual shopping was something else— and it felt oddly intense.

Anelace was good at intense sex, but intense relationships were not in her repertoire. That type of intensity had weighted one end of the standard relationship ultimatum for years—get all the way in, or get out of my bed, to quote one fed up woman. She'd broken some hearts.

For the second time in an hour, guilt pulled at her, a nagging little beastie with sharp claws.

And the fear was back. That mean little doubt that said this was fleeting, that giving a gal some orgasms and making her smile didn't mean she'd think you long-term material. Was Meidani going to turn around and say Anelace was no good other than for fun? How about when Anelace screwed up? And she would screw up.

Not that Meidani had shown any sign of being fickle.

Meidani picked up a bundle of plain white underwear.

"You'll model those, right?" Anelace whispered.

Meidani made a face at Anelace. "I promised I'd pick them up for my brother."

"Oh hells. I didn't need that image. Can you do a brain sani, doc?"

"Oh shush. You started it. Quit getting lewd about my brother's underwear, then."

Anelace adjusted her hat, trying not to grin like a fool.

They left with a bag hooked over one of Anelace's arms, and Meidani over the other. Her hand was a firm, warm weight that Anelace was swiftly getting used to.

A couple walked in front of them up curving stairs. Both wore black pants and crisp blue shirts, too clean to be weekday clothes.

It was about that time. In fine Sunday tradition, couples would be walking together through the promenade and residential quarters. The serious love birds, married or not, would be sneaking into quiet corners, inviting each other home for a Sunday snuggle.

"Where next?"

"Becky's laundry. Then the No Name."

"You don't do your own laundry?"

"I got an order coming from the synthesizer. A new dress."

"Oh, nice."

"I'll model that," Meidani allowed.

"Good." Under the guise of thanks, Anelace stole a kiss, making Meidani giggle then check no one had heard her.

It was shaping into the sort of day Anelace would never have expected. It was homey and comforting and sweet. It was a traditional Sunday afternoon courtship, complete with the traditional bizarre hat on Meidani's head.

It was nice how happy she could make Meidani just by walking. So she walked.

They took the long way around the ground floor of the promenade, passing a few more couples walking arm in arm.

Meidani held Anelace's arm and smiled warmly at the people she knew. People greeted her back and cast curious or approving glances at Anelace. Every time it happened, Anelace felt a little surge of confused pride.

Somehow, they never approached the ones sending the disapproving glances.

It was good to meet Meidani's people. Anelace wasn't friendly with any of the Sunday crowd. She'd always been more of a Friday night socializer.

When Meidani had finally collected a forgotten hair clip from the No Name and they turned for the halls to her quarters, Anelace pulled her close and murmured, "Don't think I haven't noticed what we're doing."

Meidani made a confused noise, but she kept her gaze on the wall, the floor—anywhere but Anelace.

"Do you think everyone on the station knows I'm yours yet? Maybe you should put a tag on me, just in case."

"I didn't..."

"Mmmhmm..."

"I'm sorry," Meidani said.

Anelace just laughed and nuzzled her neck. "I wasn't complaining."

Well, it hurt less than a branding. And now she knew. Maybe Anelace had been a one-night experiment at some point, but they were past that. The idea intimidated and pleased her by turns.

"It's definitely okay that I'm here?" Meidani asked.

"Yes; it's great. Better than okay. It means I'm not bored."

"And you do this every week?"

"Mostly. It let's me keep an eye on where the blobs are, where things are getting hot."

A thick, leafy green plant sat in the hall like a lost puddle of jungle. That dumb plant was Mr. Hawser's pride and joy.

Anelace poked it with a long plastic stick. The plant was as old as she was, and a bad idea, but Mr. Hawser was cussed stubborn. Maintenance had given up on making him get rid of it.

"Stand back a bit. Over there." Anelace nodded down the hall, away from Mr. Hawser's door.

Then she used the stick to give the plant a vigorous shake, tearing loose leafy bits to fall like confetti. She watched carefully, but saw nothing suspicious, even after a little poking in the dirt below.

She turned. "Okay. The playground next."

"That's it?"

"Yep. If there was anything rockward of the influx sorters up here, it would be right here. Blobs love that damn plant."

"And the owner lives out here? It has to be dangerous."

Anelace shrugged. "You'd be surprised how many people live out here. They've lived here their whole life, maybe, and get attached. Or they think it's like a battle, and they refuse to lose."

"And maintenance doesn't make them move? Or the Sheriff?"

"Sometimes they try. Mostly, folk get to make their own fool decisions."

"Try? It doesn't work?" Meidani looked highly dubious about the whole idea.

Anelace shrugged. "Phasers. Booby-traps. An illegal gun got Hoi Belse."

They walked down the corridor, heading forward and inward in the station.

Meidani had color in her cheeks and a spark in her eye. Extermination was enough excitement to fire her blood. But rounds were not so dangerous her brothers would break Anelace's bones. Hopefully. They already were making pointed remarks about Meidani coming home from dates the next morning. Sleepovers only two months after their first date? Sounded suspicious.

The two women strode down halls on the border between maintained and abandoned. The lights all worked, but some were missing sconces. The floor was spongy with spray-grip, but a rut of worn brown was forming at the center. And the wall was smudged with soot and dust thick enough to write in, in places. This hall hadn't been clean stucco with regulation flooring for at least two decades.

Meidani twined her hand with Anelace's.

They found the playground empty, but Anelace knew it was not forgotten. This was the biggest one on the station, with the best castle of hoops and bars and swing and slides.

Meidani looked around as if seeing it for the first time. "Why do people still come here? After what happened to Trish?"

"If babies don't find blobs here, they'll find them somewhere else. You can't keep people in bubbles."

"But why here? No one will live around here."

"Here isn't so bad. That's the problem. It's fine, nearly every time. Good odds turn everyone into gamblers."

Anelace slid on her gloves and started a circuit around the edge of the room, picking up thick blue safety foam tiles to peer underneath. Meidani followed, curious, but staying out of the way.

"I guess it's because it's children, and a playground. It's not adults, it's not life support systems. That's why it bugs me so much." Meidani mused.

Anelace paused. "Every person on Rosewood knows this place is awful. It's dangerous, it's dying, it's disappointing, it's mean. And every person dreams somehow it'll be different for the people they love. They'll be happy, healthy. They'll get out, go be a businessman with a fancy comm pad on a world with beaches and real sun. And in that fantasy, kids get to play at the playground.

"If they gave up on playgrounds, they'd be giving up on a lot more."

Anelace finished checking for blob damage under the flooring and began poking her stick into every crevice in the equipment. She was conscious of Meidani's eyes on her, assessing.

"My mother never let me play at the playground," Meidani said.

"Your mother has more sense than most of the folk around here."

"She let me think my father would help me leave, though."

"Genetic?" Anelace asked cautiously. The entire station knew who Meidani's sperm donor was, but no one, not even Anelace, would be the first to bring it up.

"Yeah. That rat bastard. Did I tell you about that?"

"No, I don't think so." Anelace tried to sound casual.

She bent to check the sticky trap under the slide.

"I asked him to endorse my application for schools on Verak III." Meidani said calmly. "He said he would. Then he started avoiding me. He had the station's

74

computer block my comms! His wife probably found out and said no." By the end, her calm had risen to not-so-veiled outrage.

Anelace strung that together in her mind. Verak III was a full planet, about six weeks away in a transport. It was where the doctor, Meidani's genetic father, was from. She could have gotten a visa, as his kid, and tuition at his school, most likely. If he'd endorsed her application.

She could have escaped.

"That little-dick chicken fucker."

Meidani laughed. "I guess that's more insulting than my version."

Ship's passage only cost twenty years pay, but nowhere remotely lawful let you in without a visa. For many places, the right to live there was the most expensive commodity they had, and quid pro quo with other nations was the name of that game. No one issued visas to someone from a place like Rosewood. Without a marriage or an off-station relative, there was no way to leave.

Anelace detoured to give her a hug. Meidani rolled her eyes—but returned the hug.

"I'm sorry. I always thought you would get out, when we were kids. You were the smart one."

"The application was years ago. I was just thinking on it. And Rosewood isn't so bad."

"We're checking the playground equipment for carnivorous amoeba," Anelace pointed out.

Meidani laughed again. She wasn't torn up about this. Bugged, maybe, but it was behind her. Anelace wanted to punch something on her behalf.

Oddly, a month late to the party, standing in a playground and holding a dirty stick, Anelace realized how very in love she was. Like, punch someone's father for being a jerk ten years ago in love. Eagerly look forward to errands every week in love.

"Um, Anelace?"

Anelace blinked. "What?"

Meidani was looking at her. She shook her head. "Go finish your checking, so you can kiss me."

"Yes, ma'am."

FIVE

The station farms, the official ones tasked with sustenance nutrition, were a blob's dream and Anelace's nightmare. Eight-foot high shelves stretched into the distance, two-foot wide slotted shelves holding cream-colored synthetic dirt and hundreds of bushy plants.

"You're fucking kidding me," Anelace said.

Sheriff Taledad sighed. The sheriff didn't much approve of her mouth.

"I can't see a thing." Except salad, fake dirt, and hundreds of places for a blob to hide.

Anelace yanked her gloves on. "Damn the Devil's hairy ass. How did this happen?"

The farms were supposed to be the safest place on the station, with heated vents, filtered water, talc lines and motion detectors.

"We don't know yet. But they're coming out of the water line, falling down through the sprinklers. Though that seems to have slowed down." Taledad answered.

Dick, sixty years old if he was a day, clutched a flamethrower while they chatted. He was an ornery old fart that used to be a foreman at the smelter. His knuckles were white and his gaze was darting. She hoped he didn't see a blob; he'd likely fry them all.

"How do you know it's slowed?" Anelace asked.

"We turned on the safety cameras," Taledad said.

"They work?"

"Well, it is the biggest farm on the station. It gets the good equipment."

The good equipment. A few working cameras, but hey, a sprinkler system full of deadly ooze.

"And you want me to clean it out? That's dangerous, and slow. You should just close the door, seal the air supply, and scorch the place."

Dick spoke up with a thick rasping voice. "You think we were born yesterday? We're sealing the air now. We have this covered."

Anelace glanced back at Taledad. "Then why am I here?"

Taledad had called for her, specific, hadn't he? He already had maintenance, but he'd wanted her.

"I just want you to have a look around."

"You need a tourist for a dangerous blob infestation?"

"There were fourteen people working in here. Six came out alive. Three more we can see the bodies on cameras. I want you to go in there, find the other bodies, and get a quick picture for the records. Then get your ass back out here."

"Photography doesn't sound much better than tourism."

"Tarnation, exterminator. Are you going to do this or not?"

"I just need to know, Sheriff, why you are going to pay me three times my going rate to traipse in there and take a couple photos."

"The agreement was for twice your rate."

"That was before I saw how dangerous it was."

Taledad stared at her. His face was still as granite, but his eyes burned with a deep inner fire. Then, slowly, his expression fell. He closed his eyes and reached a weary hand up, scrubbing it down his face.

"I have to go tell eight families that they have someone waiting for them in heaven now, and before I do that, I want to know that it was the blobs that did it and not the fires. I don't want any doubt. All right? I'm just sentimental like that, I guess."

"I ain't hearing this," Dick muttered.

Anelace couldn't believe she was hearing it herself. Shut down and burn out was chapter one of the company's safety procedure manual. Taledad, tasked with keeping order, should be making that priority one.

But that was the age-old question, wasn't it? When you sealed and scorched, how many deaths could a moral person blame on the blobs? On some off chance someone had survived so far, Taledad didn't want to be the one to kill them. And he was probably using his own bank account to payroll it.

Still Anelace hesitated.

It was deadly out there, and they knew she was the only one crazy enough to do it. But she wasn't a hero, she was an exterminator. She paid her taxes, she had her dignity, she ate well and she bought Meidani real flowers on Friday nights, and most of all, she got paid. She always got paid.

"Hell, just leave 'em. Wait a bit. Maybe Taledad can pay you to be the one to tell your girlfriend." Dick spoke up, sly and vicious.

"What?"

"The big one. He's still missing."

He meant Brisco. She knew he worked on a farm somewhere—pride of the family. It was a nice, safe job.

Anelace's heart sank like a rock in syrup, a heavy, sluggish feeling deep in her chest. All she could see was Meidani's face, twisted in sobs, shoulders shaking, crying for a brother who hadn't come home. The brother she bickered with and adored. It would break a part of Meidani to lose her brother.

A brother Anelace could save.

Maybe.

"You're a good-for-nothing, sick in the head mercenary. You really are." Taledad cursed. "I can do you three times the pay: 2,000 credits, one day."

Anelace pulled herself back out of her nightmare.

"Yeah. Yeah, okay. 2,000 credits," Anelace repeated, dazed. She struggled to get back into a professional head space, to be the woman who was invited here to do something other than just freak out.

All he'd had to say to get her for free was Brisco's name, but revealing that now wouldn't help anything.

She flexed her gloves hands, her back. She had her hair pulled into a tail and a carbon-cloth hood under her hat, protecting the back of her neck. It was hot and uncomfortable and she wasn't going in there without it.

Behind her, Taledad and Dick were already backing for the entrance. She'd nearly forgotten them. Anelace pulled her watch out of a pocket. It was an old-fashioned digital affair, round and gold with a tiny scratched face.

"Remember, get out of here before thirty minutes. They're going to fire it up, whether you're out or not."

She waved at Taledad that she understood, and set another alarm. Thirty minutes was the one thing she wouldn't be forgetting.

Then she strode into the room.

Tender greens swayed in artificial wind at eye height, stomach height and knee height. Damp greenery blocked her sightlines, sparkling with refractive drops.

She walked between leaves stretching like reaching hands. Water dropped from the top shelf, splatting on her hat, making her jump and swerve.

Taledad had said they came from the sprinkler system, a rain of teeny-tiny amoeba spores. It was a shower of death, when death was no bigger than the end of your pinkie.

That's what happened when a blob split in standing water for too long. That small, they would be hard to kill, impossible to avoid. But she kept walking, covering yardage in the huge farm with a ground-eating stride.

She glimpsed a flicker of blue low to the ground, an incongruity in the beige and green. Her eyes felt tight and tried to slide away from the sight, but she forced herself to look.

The rough denim of a pant leg stretched from the fallen body of a worker. His hand, flung wide, was encased in ooze. Two blobs were feeding furiously, purple-red and bulbous like a plump tick. Beneath the feeding oozes was more purple-red, the color of skin-less flesh.

His face, turned sideways against the floor, lay in a pool of escaping blood. His pants rippled as a blob climbed his leg for its favorite squishy bits.

You'd think the little blobs were too small to kill a grown man, but you'd be wrong. The pain of getting a blob on you, anywhere on you, brought most people to an incapacitated fetal position. And the blobs' flesh-eating nerve poison brought swift unconsciousness when it reached the spinal column.

She'd found the pooled remnants of a couple long-gone vagrants over the years, but never seen a fresh corpse being stripped of tissue.

For a moment, just a moment, she ignored it all and took one long slow breath. The clean smell of greenery clung to her nose. Then she pulled it together. There were four more people to find.

She raised the camera, getting a few horrifying pictures to ID the guy with. Then she ducked two aisles over and continued on a straight course for the rockward wall.

And now she saw the telltale flickers of texture. There were little spots of brown or green, a blob too stuffed with nutrients to be transparent. She turned her head to stare at the tiny shift of a slowly moving surface. The signs of a blob.

She could hear quiet rustling, plant against plant. She didn't know how much was normal, caused by the oddly strong airflow blowing across her cheeks. She didn't know if she was listening to blobs.

She calculated size and distance with each new sighting before plunging on to the next. She kept a careful mental catalogue of the death surrounding her—one behind, two up high, one approaching on the ground to her left—but she didn't slow. If she paused to kill each of the little ones, she could be there for hours. And she didn't have hours—she had about twenty-four minutes left to save Brisco's ass.

Because somehow, somewhere in the last few minutes, her goal had changed. The Sheriff thought everyone was dead, but Anelace refused to believe it. What in a fiery hell did the company know?

Anelace was going to save Brisco.

She would save him so she would never see the haunting bruise that loss would leave on Meidani's smile.

She heard an extra rustle of plant leaves, like a stiff breeze, gaining in strength. She checked her motion and turned, and saw waving plant tops in the distance. A disturbance raced towards her, too small to be a person. Too small to be damaged by a phaser.

She ran further and ducked two aisles over, alert and ready. A fluttery leaf brushed her cheek; a little tickle made her jerk away and over correct.

The attacking blob came along the ground, right up the center of the aisle behind her. It was faintly orange, as big as two fists and moved with a weird fluttering motion. It was shaped like a bullet, and moving fast like one, too.

Too fast.

Fear smacked Anelace's mind, but her grip was sure when she clawed out her pop gun.

Anelace faced it fully, planting her feet and firing squishy balls. The first flew wide, wasting time she didn't have. The second hit, a perfect strike. The sheen of kerosene coated the pulpy orange goo.

The blob still raced for her, a foot away. There was no time to ignite it.

She pulled back her boot and let fly with a solid kick. The blob lifted, punting right back down the aisle, flying through the air to splat into the floor in the distance.

Anelace ignored her ten different ways of making fire. She ignored her boot, too—that was why it was steel-lined. She pulled out a hull patch, a six-inch by six-inch square of metal fabric and glossy paper. The blob was moving in her direction again. She pulled the paper off the strong, fast-acting glue underneath.

Hull patches were meant for in-battle repairs, when you didn't have time for a proper weld.

She dropped the patch on the ground, and backed away from the returning blob. It was bruised, but not broken, and too brainless to be intimidated. Goo slid over the industrial-strength sticker, and caught, as she flicked open her firestarter.

The blob roiled, but the patch held fast to its hide, a dark grey square edged in white magnesium stitching. She flung a shower of sparks from her hand. Blue-white marks fell and dotted the blob before fading to uselessness. She tried again while she hurriedly backed up—and then a spark took, igniting kerosene. The weld line followed, sparking into blazing glory.

Anelace looked away, but not fast enough. Her vision swam with dark after-images, little ghost blobs swimming across the landscape. She stumbled further back, but the magnesium fire subsided to something more normal. The fire licked up the blob's ichor, consuming the blob's flesh at a leisurely pace.

She didn't spectate—she trotted away down the aisle, panting for air. If the fire suppression system started spitting out tiny death, she didn't need to be around to know it. As she moved, she sprinkled a little healing powder on her boot to neutralize the worst of the blob acid.

She reached the rockward wall with twenty-one minutes left, and turned to follow it.

Between one row and the next, things changed. The shelves still stood with pots still slotted in, but there were no plants and no dirt. And the pots had changed too—they were deeper, only two to a shelf. She had left the salad department behind.

With no threatening greenery leaning to brush her, her anxiety lifted a little. She stood straight, relaxing her shoulders a bit—just a bit. She wouldn't truly relax until sometime next week. This one was taking a toll.

She switched to a jog, marking the distance in her mind. She should be about a fourth of the way down the wall. She turned again, down a row, heading back for the forward wall.

There was water in the empty row, and blobs, but her passage was uneventful. The blobs cowered in the bottom of the deep tubs, soaking up moisture, or slowly oozed across the metal-grated floor. She ran until she reached the opposite wall again, too far down from the door to see it. Her search pattern was loose, but she had too much ground to cover for careful.

She followed the wall again, ticking another eighth towards the halfway point. The scenery changed another time. Now the large tubs had darker soil in them, and tiny little plants.

She turned down a row of baby plants and trotted rockward. Her neck hurt from swiveling, from staring down aisles trying to spot bodies.

She heard a loud click overhead, then a hiss. She glanced up to get a face full of misty rain. Why were the sprinklers still on?

Anelace snapped her gaze back to the ground, putting a stiff hat brim between her face and the water. A foot in front of her, a huge raindrop jiggled where it hit, unfolding into a tiny lump of transparency. Mirroring the blob, terror unfolded in her mind.

Anelace ran.

Her shirt under her vest was a thick protective blend. Her gloves, boots, and vest were solid. But the denim of her pants was minor protection, and most of her face was bare skin.

Anelace ran as the light rain continued. The sprinklers were over the rows—she was only getting the mist. It was clammy on her overheated face, and thickened the air she was rapidly breathing.

Then something heavier landed on her hat and slowly slid off the back brim. She lost track of where the blob fell, but she wasn't going to stop. She ran. She waited for the burning pain of blob burn to come, on her back or legs, but it didn't.

At the next crossover, the wide center aisle, she turned left and quickly discovered the sprinklers' area was only six rows wide. Clear of falling water, she stood and gulped air. Relief and exhaustion made her limbs weak.

Her watch showed seventeen minutes left. She'd need six to safely make it back to a door.

She walked further down the center aisle. The shelves were empty again, between crops.

And then she spotted an anomaly. In the sea of grey metal shelves, there was a gap on the rockward side. An anomaly was exactly what she was looking for.

She worked a zigzag route closer and closer to the missing shelves, until she could confirm they were toppled. Six toppled shelves, like a great bull of a man had flailed around.

Hope and fear clashed in her stomach.

Then she spotted the tubs. Two giant planting tubs, end up, lying perfectly flat on the ground. The other tubs had stayed attached to their shelves, ending up sideways wherever the shelves were thrown, but these two... Those were hiding places.

There were plenty of blobs in sight, clustered on shelving, piled underneath it, but nothing large. As she got closer she saw talc, an emergency line of the talc/lime/salt mixture that most amoeba wouldn't cross. It was spilling out from under the overturned tubs, a messy line, spilling wide in some spots.

Hope surged, but so did fear. It was a messy line, with gaps and smears. A few shriveled blobs formed a second border around it. Some could have made it through. Even if there was a person under there, their sanctuary could have become their prison as the first ooze joined them.

She knocked on one of the tubs with the butt of her phaser. "You alright in there?"

A desperate shrill voice answered with enough force Anelace took a step back. "Get us OUT! HELP US HELP US PLEASE!"

Someone lived, and she loved them for it. A fierce smile stretched her face.

Anelace used her gloved left hand to pick up little blobs from the tub—the biggest was still less than the size of her nose—and flicked them into the distance. She pushed a line of oozes away with her boot, and threw some extra talc on a half dozen little oozes slowly following behind her.

A blob had no concept of league, or how far out of theirs Anelace might be.

Then she lifted. The metal tub was surprisingly heavy, drawing a grunt from deep in her sternum.

Inside, two women were tangled, their eyes wide and faces splotchy. They'd only fit because they were small women and arranged just so. They struggled free, smearing the talc, stumbling to get up.

"Where's Brisco?" one of them asked.

Despair wobbled her knees. Was he alive? Wasn't he?

"That was my question for you," Anelace replied.

They'd been under there an hour by now, and their limbs weren't working. One woman's leg was dragging behind her—an old injury, or a new one?

A bang sounded in the direction of the other tub. Anelace turned and looked while holding up the tub for the women to finish their escape. Her hands itched for her phaser, but the women moved slowly. Slow was the best they could do.

Brisco climbed free of the second tub, looking around and stretching his back.

"Hey, exterminator," he called.

"Farmhand. How you holding up?" She kept her voice professionally neutral, because she knew she had a delighted grin on her face. They were getting out of there.

They would survive.

Unless it all went to hell.

Brisco stared into the distance, at a smudge of blue amongst all the beige and metal and green. It was another denim-covered leg, splayed on the floor. He was looking at the corpse of the fifth employee, most like.

"I could be better," he said.

Her happiness tempered. Brisco was alive, but there were still dead. The farmhands were all scarred.

Anelace looked down at her new boot, the thick synth-leather spotted with discoloration. A wide hole stretched across the toe, a hole that went right down to the steel lining at the center.

She kicked her foot around in the talc.

"I know the feeling."

Brisco was alive. Caring too much about the others would break her, but Brisco was alive. This was a win.

Her pocket watch trilled a warning. Ten minutes left.

The women were huddled near their tub, terrified of the tiny blobs slowly making their way toward them. Anelace kicked one that had gotten a bit close.

"We still need to get out of here," Anelace said. "They're gonna fire the place out. We need to get back to the entrance, but the sprinklers are still on."

Brisco pointed with his chin. "Thataway then."

Anelace rubbed the butt of her phaser for comfort. "Back in the green?"

"It's a different timer. Potatoes don't get watered today."

Potatoes. Right.

Brisco led them to the safety of a nearby door, while Anelace clutched her phaser and surveyed the greenery. She would have nightmares about greenery.

SIX

Anelace got home late that night, after the lights had been turned down and the air scrubbers turned up. Brisco and the other farmhands were home to mourn and finish realizing they'd nearly died, but Taledad had wanted his money's worth. She'd reviewed schematics and given her opinion—illegal water tap somewhere down ship. Then she'd gone with the maintenance boys to find it.

And the whole time Dick was standing there with a flamethrower and crazy eyes, scaring her more than the blobs ever did.

Meidani was in Anelace's bed, curled in a sleeping lump of naked limbs and patchwork quilts. Her hair was braided for bed and her expression was peaceful under the faint night-set lights of Anelace's quarters.

Anelace didn't want to wake her, but she was sour with worry sweat, so she shrugged off her clothes in her best silence. The air was cold and she felt restless in the adrenaline aftermath. She washed first, quiet as she could. Then she climbed into the cozy bed nook. She even thought she'd pulled it off, until Meidani spoke. "Night light off."

The lights blazed to full bright, which was very bright.

"Ouch." Sleepy Meidani threw an arm across her eyes.

"Lights off!" Anelace commanded.

Nothing happened. Anelace sighed. Meidani buried her face into a pillow, fully woken up now.

Anelace stood to use the control panel near the door.

"Bad mic?" Meidani asked.

"I think the ship's computer just hates me."

"Probably. Your heat's busted, too."

The station was originally built with every light switch and door hooked to a vast voice-activated network. Mostly, these days, the network just didn't work. Or caused messes. Or shorted things out. Even the grid on Rosewood was old and crotchety.

Anelace used her thumb on the front door panel to turn the lights off completely. The panel was a makeshift layer of medical tape with the buttons drawn back on with cheap copper wire. Panels were easy to fix. You had to buy ceiling microphones when they broke, though. Or steal them from one of the few well-policed areas where the company still replenished them.

In the cool darkness, she crawled back into bed and drew Meidani into her arms. The woken woman buried her face against Anelace's shoulder, her breath a pool of comforting heat.

Anelace slowly relaxed, carefully not remembering the way blobs had been burrowing into the eye sockets of the last corpse. Meidani's hair smelled like apples, and that was a much better thought.

Anelace was safe. Meidani and Brisco were safe. She'd been paid, and she had a soft woman in her arms. At the end of the day, when her boots were off and the lights were out, that's all that mattered.

Meidani hitched her breath, an uncomfortable catch that filled Anelace with dread. Then she started talking.

"I hate that you're an exterminator. I hate everything about it. I hate when you get hurt and I hate when you don't, because I just spent all day worrying for nothing."

Anelace lay still. She could feel gentle lips moving against her collarbone, a comforting touch, but the words she heard were chilling.

"I hate your money, your weapons and your brand new boots. I hate when you buy me things, because I know the money comes from you nearly dying." There was real venom in Meidani's voice. "I thought I could love you, just because it was you. But I can't. I hate everything about you but you."

Anelace's worry opened into a giant pit. The sure suspicion that Meidani would leave her was back and it hurt like a wound. She couldn't do life without Meidani, not anymore. That ship had left port.

"I'm sorry," Anelace whispered helplessly.

"And then today. All I can think is how happy I am that you were there. I knew you were called, that you were in there, and all I worried about was Brisco. I am happy you are so crazy you know all about saving someone from blobs. I am such a hypocrite."

Meidani swallowed a sob. "Thank you for saving him."

Anelace's heart dropped lower. She'd done this to her.

Anelace tried to speak, but Meidani's fingers pressed her lips, silencing her. Her lips followed, moving slowly in the dark.

Anelace sighed, kissing back. She didn't know what had just happened, but it scared her. Were they okay? If she broke it off with Anelace over the bounties, she wouldn't be the first—just the first to hurt. She couldn't ask, so she kissed back.

Meidani tangled her hand in Anelace's hair. Her lips were smooth against Anelace's mouth, her kiss a command. Anelace melted under her, open and pliant.

Meidani had learned Anelace's body like it had a textbook, and she used that now to coax desire awake.

Anelace reveled in the touch of Meidani's mouth. She wanted Meidani to distract herself. She wanted to be distracted as well.

Meidani's hand glided down the flat planes of Anelace's stomach, a sweet caress. Meidani paid attention, but she was impatient. Always impatient.

Anelace caught her hand and took control of the kiss. A few kisses couldn't completely chase away the horror she'd seen that day, but she had other ideas of what could.

She pressed her body against Meidani's, skin against skin. With her mouth she distracted and played and demanded, licking then retreating, nipping and sucking at Meidani's bottom lip. It was Meidani's turn to melt. Anelace pushed aside the blankets and began to explore her.

Using her fingers, her lips, even the soft skin of her cheeks and wrist, she slowly traced the curves of Meidani. She found smoothness and tiny scars, perfection and blemishes. Anelace kissed every part of her, teasing her with her tongue.

She listened to Meidani breath, barely louder than the softly whirring air scrubbers. And it was cold in there, too cold, bringing out goosebumps on Anelace's flesh.

Meidani's breasts were small mounds with chill-pointed nipples, a mere hint at the subtle curves she had when standing. Her stomach was soft and dented with shallow stretch marks. Anelace treasured that she didn't push Anelace's hands away from them, not any more. So she licked across Meidani's waist, skin bumpy under her tongue, making Meidani hiccup a little laugh.

The gentle curve of Meidani's hips, from her waist to her ass to her thighs, was some sort of perfect shape created only by nature. It fascinated her.

Anelace traced it, first with her hand and then with her lips. She dotted gentle kisses down the inside of Meidani's thigh, down her leg.

Then Anelace moved back up, drawing the blankets thick around them. Meidani was laying quiet, breathing deeply. Anelace traced the shape of her lover's lips.

Meidani sighed. A soft wind slid across Anelace's hand.

"I don't want slow. Not tonight."

Anelace understood. She didn't want to think, either.

Anelace poured distraction into an artful kiss.

The kiss didn't stay calculated for long. Meidani was greedy for touch. The kiss grew hard while their bodies stayed soft, warming again, wrapped together under the covers.

Anelace broke the kiss and rolled away. She reached beneath the bed, sliding open a cupboard and pulling out a silicone tulip. It was a toy she'd bought for Meidani the week before. When she'd opened the box, Meidani had been scandalized. But after a long night of teasing and fucking, she'd admitted out loud that she liked the ridiculously expensive tech.

I hate your money.

A sobering chill wracked Anelace's body. She strangled the memory of Meidani's words and shoved it aside.

Anelace pressed a switch on the toy flower, and it filled her hand with a slow thudding vibration. She slid it across Meidani's body, her stomach, her shoulders, letting her know what was coming. Meidani's body rocked involuntarily. Anelace kissed her again, holding her close, with the vibrator between them beating a tempo on their sternums. Then she drew away.

"Turn around, towards the wall," she whispered.

Meidani turned to her other side, facing away. Anelace lifted Meidani's hand from her side, bending her elbow for her, reaching it up. She took two of Meidani's fingers into her mouth, and sucked them slowly, listening to the comforting sound of Meidani's breath.

Then she moved the fingers to Meidani's front and down her body.

Meidani took over. She pressed her wet fingers against her clit and began to slowly move them in small circles.

Anelace wrapped around Meidani, spooning her. She flipped her braid out of the way and drew her teeth across the vulnerable skin of Meidani's neck. A little thrill jolted her, like it always did when she remembered she could do those things to Meidani now. And that she'd like it.

Meidani continued to pleasure herself, putting on a show to please Anelace. Anelace could always tell when Meidani's pleasure was for show. Meidani was heedless and needy when she thought only of herself.

Anelace's arm was around Meidani, the toy in her hand. She turned it back on and pressed it against Meidani's mons. A hesitation, then Meidani pressed her hips toward the toy, seeking penetration.

Anelace held the toy steady and closed her eyes. They did little in the darkness.

Meidani was pressed back against her body, every movement a caress to Anelace's front. Anelace's body reacted, getting warm and loose, finally relaxing a bit. Shifting again, Meidani fitted her opening to the blunt toy and began to rock her hips in exquisite little motions, helping it stretch her. It was sexy enough to kill a lesser woman.

Anelace gently sucked at Meidani's earlobe.

"Anelace," Meidani whimpered, distraught.

"Shhhh... I'm here. Fuck it."

Meidani moaned again and pressed forward until the thick toy slid deep inside her. They'd played with the tulip before, but tonight was a different sort of night. Meidani was tired and upset, and Anelace knew a good fucking would put that at bay.

Anelace turned up the vibration slightly and flexed her wrist. Meidani accepted the stretch, lifting her leg back over Anelace's, spreading herself wide.

The flower pushed into Meidani easily, her body slick. Anelace raised the vibration another notch.

Under a thick layer of blanket, their bodies intertwined. Anelace was beginning to sweat, a good sweat.

In the close darkness she couldn't see her lover, and that was her only regret. She could hear her, though, and feel her pressed close. She could taste her.

Meidani's breath sounded faster, puffs of air in the night. Her body was warm, emanating heat in a way that did more to warm Anelace than a blanket ever could. The tulip in Meidani still vibrated, dulling to a faint buzz in Anelace's hand. And the wetness of her body grew with each thrust of her demanding hips, making messy, sexy noises Anelace loved and Meidani would be embarrassed by if she noticed them.

Meidani's fingers fumbled across Anelace's hand, moved to her own clit, pressing a circle. Her motions were faster now, hurried with need. Each catch and sigh filled Anelace's world—that, and the thick weight of the flower in her hand. When Meidani moaned, Anelace rewarded her by turning up the vibration another notch.

"Anelace..."

Meidani moaned her name, a begging sound, and Anelace sighed pleasure. She kissed the writhing woman's shoulder, her neck, tasted her sweet skin.

Meidani's noises weren't gentle anymore. She was gasping for breath, groaning and whimpering. She was chasing an orgasm like it was trying to escape.

She remembered nothing of her earlier words, and that was how Anelace wanted it. If Meidani forgot everything, maybe she would forget any hint of the goodbye Anelace was scared she'd heard.

Anelace slid her other arm beneath Meidani, gathering the moaning woman tightly against her. She moved her hand faster, a rolling fucking motion, and Meidani moaned approval. She begged, and the words echoed in the dark. Meidani's own hand moved quickly on her clit. Her hips jerked to meet the toy.

Anelace fucked her and cradled her until she came. Meidani jerked and tensed in her arms, and moaned a long growl of completion. Her body, still tense, shuddered and her head bent back to lay against Anelace's shoulder.

Anelace switched off the toy while Meidani twitched in her arms. Anelace slowly removed the tulip. In a few short moments, the toy had gone from too much to not enough and back to too much. And Meidani had gone from angry to needy. Could she come around to relaxed?

"Anelace..." Meidani murmured.

"Mm, baby?"

Meidani didn't answer, her breath slowing. Anelace continued to hold her, and closed her own eyes and drifted.

Meidani couldn't break it off. Anelace wouldn't know what to do with herself without Meidani to check up on, to chat with, to fuck silly. Meidani couldn't fall in love with her because she worried too much about her death, but maybe she wouldn't leave her. Maybe.

"Anelace..."

"Mmm?"

"If I fall asleep without cleaning up, I'll regret it in the morning."

"Shhh. No, you won't."

Meidani just laughed like Anelace had told her life was easy or gravity a myth. Then she disentangled herself, and went to unfold the sani.

Anelace fell asleep, Meidani's earlier tears beating out ooze-dissolved flesh for a place in her nightmares.

SEVEN

The Olive Branch was your friendly neighborhood bar, or would be if you were a twitchy space-fried gun for hire or a meat-sack working ship security. The walls were drab olive, the furniture utilitarian black metal. The lighting near the bar was good, but the far corners faded into shadow. And it always smelled of whiskey and gun oil.

Anelace sipped her drink on a low stool near the center of the chipped black bar.

There'd been a cleanup bounty. Cleanup bounties came before a visit from some human rights activist, checking whether the company took care of its sheeple in this god-forsaken hole.

Cleanup bounties were good fun. Even the kids joined in, preteens hunting in small groups wielding torches and pliers, running down the halls, checking under grates for little squishies. Adults looked on fondly or in horror, depending on their sensibilities.

Anelace had wandered far afield then paid Meidani's youngest brother to stand in the long bounty line for her. He hadn't been hunting with the packs himself, proving yet again his mother was the smart one roundabouts.

Anelace had concentrated on cleanup, setting traps and netting small ones by the dozen. She spent the whole two days reinforcing her boundaries around the infected areas, pushing blob presence back into the abandoned areas and away from residents.

It was the first bounty in three years she'd finished with no injuries. Now she was killing time until Meidani got off work, hoping to be rewarded for her pristine health.

While time ticked, she idly listened to two weapons techs at a nearby table debate the effectiveness of hull-mounted projectiles.

That's what she'd wanted to be as a kid—a weapons tech or gunner. As an adventurous little girl in pigtails with a rat-bastard father and a lot of anger, she'd dreamed of firing the big guns on a freighter. She'd fantasized about vaporizing pirates and space junk, and going anywhere but Rosewood. Well, she'd been young.

The bartender bobbled his eyebrows at Anelace, catching her attention. Behind her, the room changed volume, getting a little quieter. She turned to see what the entire bar was focused on.

Meidani crossed the floor. She wore the jeans she claimed didn't fit anymore, blaming her cookie discount at the No Name. Her shirt was pink gingham, bunched at her breasts, with capped sleeves. Her hair was gathered back under a matching scarf. She was wrapped like candy, both pretty and cute. Anelace immediately wanted to unwrap her.

Meidani smiled when she saw Anelace, an open expression this place didn't often see, and she walked for the bar. Heads throughout the room turned to follow her.

She was a sex kitten among tigers. Every scarred veteran in the room had an eye on her ass, and she hadn't even noticed.

Anelace began to laugh.

"What?"

"Nothing, really," she kissed Meidani's cheek. "You're looking amazing tonight."

Meidani glanced down at her clothing, reminding herself what she had worn. And Anelace realized Meidani was alone, no brother in tow, walking around the roughest level of the promenade. One more flight of stairs and it was the brothels.

Anelace downed her whiskey and stood, sliding her arm around Meidani's very pleasant waist. "Let's get out of here."

And just like that, Meidani's expression went from nice to fierce. Oops.

"I thought we could have a drink out tonight. You're celebrating, right? You'd rather do that alone? Or with someone else?" Her voice dropped menacingly at the end.

In hindsight, Anelace saw exactly how she'd screwed up, but she couldn't regret her words. Damn Meidani was hot when angry.

"Of course not. I was waiting to celebrate with you. I just didn't realize you were off already." Anelace slid her finger along the ridge of Meidani's ear, willing her to be soothed. A night of the two of them, somewhere nicer, would be perfect. She ignored the rest of the room, ignored the hard glares from people twenty-five light years away from their wives. This wasn't a bar for happy couples.

Meidani removed Anelace's hand from her ear. "But you always celebrate here. It's tradition."

Meidani fixed her with the steely glare of a hopped up bravo. The angry glitter in her eyes was at odds with the pink gleam of her lip gloss. And that was why Anelace was in love with her.

Meidani wasn't going anywhere until she wanted to leave.

"How about we move down, then?" Anelace suggested.

Meidani let herself be led to the end of the bar.

The bar met the wall in an L shape, the over-painted metal held in place by industrial rivets. The end was a good spot, with a decent view of the room, but dark enough to let them sit unnoticed. Hopefully.

As they walked, Anelace catalogued the room. Visiting spacers she'd dismissed were now possible threats—never mind that they were just eating and joking about "the boss." If Anelace had a credit for every fistfight she'd seen break out over simple jokes, she could retire.

Meidani slid onto a stool, sweeping her gingham-wrapped hair to one side so she wouldn't sit on it. The rest of the women in the room, Anelace included, were wearing dark colors with plenty of pockets for weaponry.

"Are you sure I couldn't take you somewhere a little safer? I love that you're celebrating with me, but this isn't really your sort of crowd."

"Anelace, I've already listened to the 'my sort of crowd' talk once today, from my mother. If you want to act like her, I guess you can, but I have a little tip for you: I don't sleep with my mother."

Anelace winced, and winced again as that image hit her. Then she started to laugh. Meidani wrinkled her nose before she laughed too.

That laugh drew looks; it always did. It also inspired smiles. The man in the corner, alone at a table, a visiting spacer with a limp and the deadly glare of a man determined to hit pension kicking, chuckled into his beer, though he probably hadn't heard what they said.

Right. Date night at the Olive Branch. What could possibly be odd about that?

"So, what did your mother say?"

Meidani sighed. "I need a drink. A whiskey."

She waved at the bartender, a towering man that used to be the Sheriff on station. Then he'd raised his bribe prices a time too many, and priced himself right out of office. "Two whiskeys." She looked at Anelace. "Neat?"

"Bitter."

"Two bitter whiskeys."

The bartender swallowed a smile, but the joke was on him. That sort of drink suited Meidani's palette fine; it was Anelace that preferred apple brandy or fruit wines. They just never had any here.

"I don't want to talk about it."

"Okay. You're okay, though? You seemed upset." Bitchier than a badger in a traveling zoo, but Anelace was too smart to say that.

"I'm fine. I'm… it's just…" Meidani took a deep breath, and started talking about it anyway. "My brothers like you now. They say you'd be useful to have in the family, and no one wanted me to marry a miner anyway. But mom decided to give me The Talk."

"Okay."

"You wouldn't understand."

"Okay."

"You promise you won't be mad at her? She's just protective. It's how she thinks."

"Okay."

"She thinks you'll take advantage of me. She says I'm too nice and you're too… something."

Anelace hid her face in her whiskey. A chill of foreboding skirted down her spine.

"She says I'll be miserable married to a woman who knows all the criminals. She says you're not our kind of people. She says she likes you, but you're not really a professional thinker."

Words stabbed Anelace, but Meidani was only turning the knife. She could count off all the ways Meidani's mother was right on her fingers. Criminals? Check. Not high class nor responsible? Check. Not big on thinking? Check.

Anelace wanted to swallow the pain and defend herself, but she also wanted to disappear. Would she make Meidani miserable? Maybe. Would Meidani's mother be the best person to know? Maybe.

But words were tumbling out of Meidani's mouth and her cheeks were stained by an outraged flush. Her tone made it obvious she didn't agree with any of it.

Anelace also wanted to be worthy of that trust, somehow.

"She might be right about that. You might be miserable." She couldn't lie, but she changed the subject. "Um, married?"

"Yeah, I didn't say that word. She jumped to conclusions." Meidani fiddled with her drink. "You're not mad, are you?"

"No, I'm not mad." And she really wasn't. If anything, she respected Meidani's mother more for saying it. "I think she forgot lesbian and fast, though."

Meidani ducked her head and sipped her whiskey.

"Or maybe she didn't," Anelace laughed and leaned over to whisper conspiratorially, "Did you tell her that's your favorite part?"

Meidani blushed and looked for eavesdroppers. She tracked the bartender for a minute before she answered, "Yes."

Anelace laughed, and laughed some more. She hadn't expected that. Sometimes she thought Meidani was the real troublemaker, between them.

Meidani started to laugh, too.

And their laughter washed away her fear, the way it did every time. If she could make Meidani this happy, how could their relationship be wrong?

A weight lifted, she got back on topic, "Your mother is right. I'm not a thinker."

"You're smart. You're one of the smartest people I know."

"But I don't think. I'd rather react, to do, not to think. Your mother was an accountant for the company, right? I couldn't do that."

"I'm a bar wench."

"You're a thinking bar wench. You don't do stupid stuff, not like I do."

They let a moment of silence stretch.

"Feel better?"

"Yes. Thank you. It's odd how that works."

Meidani glanced around. A server had started shift, bringing fried turnips out to a table of men still in silver and blue Kao-Petersen security jumpsuits. They all looked about old enough to shave, but their phasers could rattle a noggin just fine.

"Not many stationers here, are there?"

"Not too many. Sometimes that new deputy, or one of the Valdez twins. And sometimes Celeste."

"Are they all killers, or just most of them?"

She said it in a joking voice, mocking the old biddies that hissed just that at Sunday dinner. But her eyes had that look, the date with a fast girl, hunting blobs, being dangerous, cheap thrill look. Anelace wanted to teach her exactly how fun being a bad girl could get.

Meidani's scarf was sagging on her hair. Her wrists were crossed on the bar, one hand tracing the lip of her whiskey.

Anelace swallowed lust, and remembered the question. "Maybe all. They get the veterans, in here."

Meidani was surprised by that, but she just nodded. Then she changed the topic to shortbread—did Anelace want some? She was making a batch soon.

The bar was getting busier, a little at a time. She kept a subconscious awareness of who entered, who left, and who moved. Partially she used her eyes and ears, and a lot of it was sheer instinct.

Then a new group walked through the door, and one guy in particular she immediately labeled Problem. The guy hadn't done a thing wrong, yet, but he rang her instincts like a dinner bell.

It was a group of four men. They wore black synth mesh and leather, practically standard-issue in this bar, but the shoes of miners—pointed boots with fashionable slick soles. They clomped. They had no pockets. They were your average group of miners pretending they were dangerous. They were bullies palling around with soldiers, and mostly earning dirty looks.

As the group crossed the room for a table dead center, she paid extra attention to the Problem, without fully looking at him. His hair was close cut, and his hands were busted up—scars and split knuckles, with one finger oddly short.

She and Meidani were still having their moment, flirting like best friends and lust-struck strangers at the same time, but Anelace kept tracking him.

Meidani was enjoying herself, her cheeks flushed and her eyes bright. She was still getting a thrill out of this, being in the rough part of town, on a date with the wild girl. Six months ago, Anelace would have said Meidani was immune to that attraction, but she'd have been wrong. And she hadn't mentioned her mother in 20 minutes.

Anelace hesitated just a minute longer. Meidani would never buy Anelace's gut feeling. She'd leave, but she'd think she was being coddled. And it wasn't nothing—Anelace knew to trust her instincts—but it was probably nothing involving them. So she turned her attention back to Meidani's story.

"And Issa told him, right there in front of everyone, maybe if he'd lay off the drinking for a few day's he could make his thingy work at night."

Anelace sputtered. "Thingy?"

"That wasn't the point of this story."

"Really? Thingy? Did she call his penis a thingy, or did you?"

Now Meidani studied her whiskey again. There were two perfect rings of condensation on the black-painted bar. "No, she said..."

"Dick? Cock?"

"Pistol."

Anelace shook with laughter. "Whore's blue balls. She didn't."

"She did! I would rather I'd never repeated that. Pistol? Why? I don't want to know about Jed's penis, but especially not his pistol."

"God, stop saying it."

"I said thingy to protect you!"

From the other end of the bar, they heard a cry of "For the cash!" It was a mercenary toast, so cliché it was used as a joke more than a celebration. The group of miners were toasting. One of them was so drunk he kept missing his friend's glass, reducing all of them to roaring laughter.

The Problem's little group had just made a joke mocking mercenaries in a room full of mercenaries. Yep, they could go now.

Meidani turned to look toward the noise, turned her attention back to Anelace. And all of Anelace's hopes that the Problem was someone else's problem fell down.

The man tugged an imaginary hat at Meidani, too slow, and missed her gaze. But he saw Anelace looking at his reflection in the mirror behind the bar.

Anelace kept her reaction off her face and turned her head so he couldn't read her lips. "We should be going."

Meidani paused, noting her abrupt concern, and God love her, went along. "So soon?" she murmured, but she stood up, leaving her whiskey unfinished. Maybe it was the fake smile straining Anelace's face that let her know something was wrong. Anelace slid some local credits across the bar, shielding the movement with her body.

A beat later and a man's tenor spoke beside them. "Hello, ladies."

Meidani nodded, her hollow work smile flickering across her lips. "Hello."

Anelace smiled too, her best Hale Fellow Well Met, a good greeting with not an ounce of sexuality. She'd figured this dance out early, around when she'd realized she'd rather be dipped in cooling tailings than marry one of the men tromping through the station. You could turn them down, sure, but not too flat, or the asshole might come out swinging.

Though sometimes, when she was spoiling for a fight, she would turn them down right proper. For example, this guy looked like he'd be fun to reject. Not with Meidani standing between them, though.

"Somewhere important to be? Or did you just need someone to buy you a drink?"

The poor-as-dirt child in Anelace wanted to flash some cash defensively, but adult Anelace comforted herself with a blank expression. She remembered how fat her bank account still was with her recent bounties. She was living large. She was treating her steady girlfriend to overpriced whiskey. She bought her own damn drinks.

She smiled a little more, but not too wide, and a little more vacant. "Oh sorry, we did need to head out. We're heading to a vid."

Vids had start times.

It was hard not to touch Meidani protectively, but she restrained herself. Some assholes, this type of asshole, could turn into a real bastard when they realized the two pretty girls were together.

"You couldn't stay? It's been a real hard run here. A man needs some time with people after too long in cold space."

Uh huh. More like he was suffering the loneliness of a mining ship with three hundred people on it. There was no such thing as a small mining ship.

Meidani shook her head, affecting a remorseful but noncommittal expression. She'd played this game before as well, probably at work.

"Aww, a little thing like you won't even take pity on me? I'm not some jerk, honey. I'm an upstanding guy. I'm a farmer, back home. Big plot of land, planet land."

Yeah, right.

Anelace hovered, not willing to turn her back on him, needing Meidani to lead the way out. And Meidani got the hint. She spoke, "No, sorry. We were just going."

Then Meidani ducked ahead of Anelace, walking for the door.

"Shame, that. Damn shame."

The guy was letting them go. One step, two, three... They were halfway to the door when his voice raised again.

"Honey, you forgot your scarf."

Meidani's hands flew to her head, and she turned.

Anelace's neck was itching, her hands were itching, her thoughts were itching. Things were about to go straight to hell, she knew it, and she had no idea how she knew it.

"I'll get it," Anelace said, but Meidani had stopped. Anelace stood as well, silently willing her to wave off the scarf.

They were halfway to the door, taking a route near the wall to avoid the guy's friends. They were surrounded by widely spaced tables, mostly big six-seaters.

The guy trotted up, holding out the flirty pink scarf. Meidani reached for it, but his hand retreated in front of her.

"Here you go." He stepped too close, reaching up to drape the scarf over Meidani's head in a useless parody of how she'd been wearing it.

"Thanks," Anelace grinned harder, but she doubted the expression was very nice.

Meidani nodded. "Yeah, thank you."

The guy's hand fell, his knuckle gently falling across Meidani's cheek, a tender gesture some women would kill to get from a supposedly landed miner. Anelace watched the moment Meidani's mood went from placid annoyance to real fear. Her body froze and her eyes went wide. Her lips nearly closed, with just a glimpse of her pearly teeth showing through.

A ghost spasm twitched Anelace's hand toward the phaser she wasn't carrying. She poured her self-control into not attacking the dickbag, not proving Meidani's mother right about Anelace's thinking. But if he touched her again, merciful God, she would kill the son of a bitch.

Blazes, this was why Meidani was escorted everywhere. So she didn't have to deal with this crap.

But the man scented her fear, and struck.

He stepped full up to Meidani, rubbing his body against her, reaching for her hair. "Stay, baby."

Anelace moved, catching his hand before it could tangle, and bringing her fist right behind it. She broke his nose with a satisfying crunch, but she didn't stop to admire his new shape. She kept pushing him, another punch to his face, a knee to his groin, pushing him off balance, away from Meidani.

He let himself be herded, gasping and trying to double over. A pain wuss. Nice.

Meidani backed up, three steps for the wall, her hand rising to touch her throat. The fear in her eyes was a two-tap to Anelace's emotions—a shot of pain, a shot of rage.

Anelace backed off the guy though. A couple punches, well, he deserved that. The bar's security cameras would exonerate her. Kicking him while he was down would get the sheriff dragging her in.

Two chairs scraped the floor. The drunk was still laughing maniacally. His friends stood slowly, sharing looks, weighing options. They were sheep, or jackals. They thought as a pack and the big thinker was still clutching his face, holding himself upright on a chair.

Then the Problem himself stood back up, roaring with affected rage. In his own version of this story, he was pretending he'd done that immediately. Only the onlookers knew he'd stood around for a half minute trying not to cry.

His posse got with the program, walking fast now.

Anelace moved to the middle of a nice open space. The worn brown carpet under her feet had stains to suggest why the space was there.

"You going somewhere, bitch?" the Problem wheezed.

One of his friend's hooted like an overexcited monkey.

From the corner of her eye she saw Meidani moving, walking slowly for the door. That was a good call.

But Anelace was nice and involved, and too far from the door for a hasty exit. "I'm right here, neighbor. Enjoying the view."

Blood flowed from the guy's smashed nose.

Confident Meidani had enough of a head start, Anelace backed off, a step here, a step there. The door wasn't far, but there were a dozen tables between here and there. This place was built for another age when the station got more traffic.

All four men surged forward, surrounding their leader, clustering too close to each other. One of them picked up a chair, throwing it at her in a not-very-impressive show of strength.

Anelace sidestepped, using those reflexes she was so proud of to be nowhere near where the chair landed. She just let it bounce.

None of these men moved with the lethal grace of an actual pro badass. They weren't the sort of hardcore killers that came through here sometimes.

The barkeep was talking to the panel behind his bar, calling for the law or maybe just his brother. The rest of the patrons were drinking up, keeping an interested eye on the scene.

As the group got close to her they maneuvered. The head asshole in charge fell back, letting his buddies take the risks, and another of his smarter friends slowed too. They were upon her, but only two of them were in close range.

Anelace ducked a punch, and took another to the torso from a guy six inches too far away to be throwing it. She bobbed and crunched her fist into someone's jaw socket, feeling a definite rearrangement.

Adrenaline surged through her, slowing time, easing her worries into something a bit more aggressive.

And she moved backward, keeping light on her feet.

The jaw guy went down, but now the overextended guy was too close. It was the drunk guy. He even smelled drunk, sour beer and old vomit. He grabbed her arm, one big hand tangling in her shirt. She grabbed his neck by the nape and pulled, helping him overbalance.

Her knee drove into his stomach once, twice. He changed his mind about grabbing her and tried to punch, but now he was too close for that. She pulled him forward again, and slammed both of her joined hands down on his kidney area as he fell.

She winced and ducked, remembering the other two, sure someone was about to hit her.

A punch landed on her ribs, swung wide around the falling guy, and pain followed. But her arm swung smoothly, her breath pulled normally. It was nothing.

Her lips were pulled back from her teeth in a joyous maniac's grin.

The drunk miner threw himself after her, full commitment, a big slab of flying flesh. She just kept moving, putting a wide table between them. One of the jackasses followed, tangling himself in a chair like he wasn't sure how feet worked.

The Problem still stood a few feet out of reach, letting his followers be cannon fodder.

This wasn't a fight; it was a comedy show. Anelace laughed in frustrated relief.

She looked at the bartender again.

He didn't look amused—his scowl was visible from across the room. He waved at her, a concussion phaser in his hand. Then he hit a button on the wall.

Klaxons sounded. He'd rigged the fire alarm. Behind her, a bulkhead would be descending to cover the door and contain the imaginary fire.

She feinted forward like she was going to kick the guy on the ground, and changed her motion into a turn. She ran for the door and ducked under it. Outside, she stood ready to bust the first head that followed her through.

Beside her, Meidani stood waiting. Her scarf lay forgotten on the ground by her feet. Her eyes were huge with shock, and she was staring right at Anelace.

By now the emergency door was at about waist height. Anelace hoped someone came through. She'd always wanted to apply her boot to someone's face.

But they didn't chase.

Anelace glanced back at Meidani and blew out a long breath. "You okay?"

"I'm fine." Meidani said primly. She bent to pick up her scarf. "And you sure had fun."

EIGHT

The room was crackling with silent awkward while the station's official doctor ran an imager up Anelace's side. He kept checking his handheld and grimacing; he was probably grimacing because he was wrong about her ribs being broken.

She had a deep red-black bruise blooming out from the knuckle print on her side, but that's all it was. She knew what a broken rib felt like, and this wasn't it. Fractured, maybe.

Meidani sat in an extra chair, grimly observing the proceedings. Her lips were pressed tightly together.

The room itself was a snug cubby in the governance block, upstairs and far forward. It wasn't as large as Meidani's storeroom, nor as clean, but it did look like a proper hospital. Chrome and white dominated the room, and there were drawers and cabinets to hold a wealth of supplies.

Yes, Anelace had suggested maybe Meidani could take a look herself, and they wouldn't need to see the doctor. Meidani had grimly responded that Anelace took Meidani's skills for granted, and Meidani would never be patching up Anelace again. And the metaphorical bruise from that hurt more than her ribs did.

Maybe Meidani's anger would cool and she'd change her mind on that, but now wasn't the time to press. Not when her usual calm was such an obvious facade.

The doctor switched to the other side, pulling at Anelace's shirt. With her shirt halfway up, he paused, glancing at Meidani.

Anelace's lips quirked. "It's nothing she hasn't seen before, Doc."

He winced. He had been trying very, very hard to ignore Meidani's existence before he slipped up. Meidani gave him a chilling glare, and everyone went back to silence.

For once, the big drama in the room wasn't even Anelace's injuries. Meidani hated her father, and her father was the good doctor. Anelace was the impetus for this unfortunate reunion.

He had a grim, demanding wife, a woman who'd come to the station with him. That wife was not Meidani's mother. Meidani's mother had never demanded support payments, never pointed a finger. The only thing they had ever asked for was help getting Meidani into an off-station medical school, and he hadn't come through on that.

"You just have a bad bruise on your ribs here. You need to take it slow. I'll give you an injection to lessen the swelling and marks, but I'm sure you've seen worse."

"What are you giving her?"

The doctor didn't even turn, didn't even try to answer Meidani's question.

Behind him, hurt anger sparked, twisted Meidani's face. It tore at Anelace's heart. And she had no idea how to fix it. A brief fantasy of twisting the guy's head around and making him address his daughter captured her mind.

And then the door opened up and in walked the Sheriff. His badge was shiny, his mustache neatly trimmed, and his boots worn. All three of them turned.

"Howdy," he tipped his hat at Meidani first.

Meidani just stared at him, and Anelace stared at her. It was by far the rudest thing Anelace had ever seen her do.

The doctor spoke angrily. "This is an exam room."

"My apologies, Doc. I can come back when you're done. When do you think you'll be done?"

The doctor hesitated. His gaze flicked to Meidani then back to the Sheriff. "We're done."

"Well, then I need to talk to Anelace."

The doctor walked out without a goodbye. Meidani made no move to leave.

After the Sherriff watched him go, he slanted a look at Meidani. That was the worst kept secret on the station, and then some.

"I saw the security tape." He said.

"Come on, Taledad, you know I couldn't let him touch her like that. You know those guys. It would only get worse."

Anelace had been practicing her "don't throw me in jail" pitch in her mind.

"I know that. I knew that before I even saw the tape. A pretty girl, a rowdy bar, and the station's resident white knight? But now I've got four assholes who got their ass kicked by one hellcat woman. A stationer."

The Sheriff threw Anelace's vest at her. Anelace, already stiffening, didn't get her hand up in time to catch it. The thick fabric smacked her in the face.

The smack made Meidani smile for the first time in an hour. Anelace couldn't even be mad at Taledad about it.

"You know what they'll do tomorrow night? They'll go out spoiling for a fight. Tomorrow, what do you want to bet me someone gets badly hurt? Maybe someone dies?"

"They were looking for trouble tonight, too. Why are you trying to blame that on me?"

The Sheriff shook his head. "Maybe you could just try a little harder to stay out of trouble. How many times have you nearly died this week?"

"Funny hearing you say that," Meidani shot back. "Considering you had her risking her life just the other day."

The Sheriff was shocked. Maybe he'd never heard Meidani speak so forcefully before—or heard her speak at all. She was talkative enough with Anelace, but that was the exception.

"That wasn't a brawl."

"That was trouble. She could have died. They both could have died, both of them at once."

Both Anelace and the Sheriff knew Meidani was referring to Brisco.

"She doesn't even work for the station and you've got her chasing blobs and nearly dying. How do you do that? Why does she do this stuff for you?"

"She'd be doing it no matter what. You and I both know your girl will save people. Her savior urge is as big as the Pastor's."

Anelace snorted. Yeah, right. If she had a hero complex, she'd be working at the pittance wages that maintenance got.

The Sheriff shifted his attention back to Anelace. "What I want to know is what Meidani was doing in that place. Are you dragging her into your trouble Anelace? Her brothers aren't going to let you off easy on this one, nor her mama."

"We were having a drink, celebrating," Anelace adopted the exaggerated homey drawl of the Sheriff. "It's right customary for the young folk around here to go out of a night and enjoy some spirits when they're in high fettle."

The Sheriff's breath eased out in an annoyed hiss. "At the Olive Branch?"

Anelace grimaced. She agreed that Meidani shouldn't have been there, and that was making it hard to argue. But she sure wasn't going to admit she'd been humoring her girlfriend.

The Sheriff tried again on Meidani. "Young lady, I know your mother will say this to you too. You don't have to be pulled into Anelace's rowdy ways. Just don't let her take you to these places. You can talk some sense into her."

Meidani chose her words carefully. "I don't think—"

The Sheriff leaned forward, opening his mouth to interrupt her, and Anelace stood up from the table with an objection on her lips. Not hearing Meidani's words when she went to all the effort of talking to you was the deepest kind of hurt you could inflict on her.

But Meidani didn't let either of them get a word in. She raised her voice and talked right over him, over Anelace, practically yelling. "I don't think you have any clue what you're talking about, or any right to say the things you do. You think you're my mother? Well, you aren't."

The Sheriff looked like he'd been smacked in the face by a flying shoe.

"Are you here to say Anelace was wrong to not let that guy just hump on me like that? Cause if you are, I think you need to worry about your how you're going to keep your job." Wow. Wow, that was a straight up threat of her family's power, her mother and stepfather's connections both, and far too crass for Meidani. "And if you're not here to say that, I don't see why you are here."

Meidani walked past him, opened the door, and held it imperiously for Anelace. Anelace glanced at her, glanced at Taledad... then she scurried her ass out the door.

They left the office, heading to find a lift. This far forward, lifts mostly worked. And they walked back to Anelace's place.

By the feel of Meidani's silence, she was fuming.

"What are you thinking?" Anelace asked softly.

"You're an idiot." Meidani replied just as quietly. "I'm thinking he's right, that you think you're a big white knight, which is exactly what my mama thinks I need. But I don't need that. And I'm thinking my mom is right. You're going to break my heart and the only thing I can do about that is break it now before you die on me."

It hurt, the last bit. It was truth and everything Anelace wanted to deny at once. She wouldn't agree. She couldn't disagree.

"And I'm thinking you enjoyed tonight. I was scared to death. I thought I might pee myself, I really did, and you were grinning like a fool." Meidani's voice was watery with emotion. "You're like a drunk. You have these stupid ideas, but they'll get you what you're addicted to, and so you think they're great ideas. And for you, you crave trouble."

Anelace's fears quietly slid to the cold, painful surface of rock bottom. This was everything she was scared of, from the crying to the final tone in Meidani's voice.

"Yes ma'am." She finally answered.

Anelace slouched low in a rear pew, listening to the Pastor at the front of the church with half an ear. He stood under a green arch, behind a podium affixed with a cross, in an acoustic shell. He addressed a large crowd, rows and rows of stationers in scarred wooden pews. The ceiling above them was high, with lights shining bright to illuminate the parishioners' hope.

At the back of the room, Anelace's hope was an angry glower and eyes squinting against the ridiculous brightness.

It had been four days, and Anelace still hadn't heard from Meidani. She'd tried hard to contact her, too—messages, a note, stopping by her house. She'd even stopped by the No Name once and fled when Lupe told her to get lost. Anelace was being ignored. That growing certainty had been drill bits of despair burrowing into her heart since yesterday.

The Pastor was talking about the wealth of family and the worldly duties that led to heaven. It wasn't as uplifting as he meant it to be. Anelace wasn't going to Heaven. She cursed, she drank, she had no family. You didn't do well in the next world unless you made a good mark in this one.

The closest she'd come was Meidani, but if she was still refusing to acknowledge Anelace after four days, it was over. Meidani was a deliberate person. She didn't throw tantrums; she made decisions.

Further up, Meidani sat in a line with her family, filling the pew that had been unofficially reserved for them for the past ten years. Mei's dress was proper, starched white printed in little red poppies. She was a beacon of serenity. Her hair was braided, a simple twining rope down her back, with a cute red bow at the bottom. It was a church dress—proper clothing no one wore on a weekday. It was the sort of thing Anelace loved removing the minute she got the other woman behind closed doors.

As the Pastor spoke uplifting words, Anelace's spirit wallowed in remorse. The hangover probably wasn't helping, either.

Eventually the sermon ended, and the congregation stood in a rustle of slacks and dresses. Even the poorest, most skinflint mine-rat didn't wear jeans to church.

Anelace tugged self-consciously at her own jeans, and slipped through the crowd in a straight line for the door. She'd changed her mind. She didn't want Meidani to see her, though that was the original reason she'd come to Sunday service.

She walked a dozen steps before Mrs. Blywigg stopped her. She asked when Anelace was coming back by the tea shop, and wasn't it so sweet that a young thing like her enjoyed a good tea?

Anelace mumbled something polite and walked out the door, into the wide hallway beyond. There, she was stopped by a concerned mother. She was wondering if the communal hall area in residential section 218B was safe enough for her boys' new fort.

Further down the hall, Meidani stood while her stepfather discussed with the mayor. And the mayor listened right back.

When Anelace reached for the stars, she went for the brightest one, didn't she? Four days, and it was already hard to remember how they'd come together, why Meidani had ever wanted Anelace.

Sheriff Taledad clapped her on the back with vigor, interrupting her treacherous brain. "Hey, exterminator. You found God, or you found your girl?"

There were blobs, even miners, she'd rather converse with than a cheerful Sheriff, at least today.

His eyes narrowed in something like concern, looking her up and down. "You doing okay?"

"I'm fine. Just heading out."

"Well, give me a second now. I've been coming by your quarters, but you're never there."

"Yeah? Life keeps me busy."

"Speaking of busy," he said, "You know maintenance has got an opening down there, right? The company just upped the pay grade too, with all the blob problems we've been having."

"Maintenance always has an opening. The company pays janitor wages to wield flamethrowers."

"Well, that's why I thought of you. You're handy with a flamethrower. It'd be safer than the bounties, when you don't have to go after the big ones on your own. And you could set up a plan, give the other guys some advice."

"And I could make janitor wages?"

Taledad pinched at his nose. "You know, if you called in sick during a bounty, and maybe some kid brought in nuclei that day, no one's going to question that. I bet you could boost your wages."

Behind Taledad, Meidani's family was heading down the hall, with her at the center of the well-turned-out group. Her dress hung to her calves, primly too long. It made her legs look shorter than they were.

She was beautiful.

Anelace drug her attention back to the Sheriff.

"I'll think on that."

Then she put her hat back on her head so she could tip the brim at him. She was already forgetting what he had to say, and Meidani was gone, ambling down the hall with the flow of the crowd.

Anelace got out of there before the next fool person wanted a favor.

NINE

Eight thousand six hundred credits waited for her somewhere on this smelly second-rate courier ship. She just had to find the last of its blob infestation and kill it.

Anelace was in the galley, a long room too small for a stationer's comfort. There were two tables that folded into the walls and a giant nutrient dispenser at one end. The walls were dented white plastic; the vents were round holes missing their grates. Real food was conspicuously absent—the crew relied on the occasional station meal for that.

She was starting to hate this ship. She already hated its captain.

The reason for her bad mood was still pulsing gently in a bowl of mushed pea soup on the table. She'd thought she'd cleaned this place out, but a six-inch wide blob had showed up overnight to prove her wrong. Problem was, if even one little straggler showed up in the month of travel after she cleaned out the ship, her payment wasn't leaving escrow. The happy little blob in soup looked a lot like eight thousand six hundred credits evaporating into thin air.

A lot had been evaporating on her lately.

Anelace flipped the bowl into a scarred metal firebox, added a squirt of volatile starter fluid, pushed the loose lid into place and set the contents on fire. It wouldn't do to melt the ugly plastic decor.

She'd spent the last couple weeks bouncing back and forth between frenetic activity and moping after Meidani. She'd written a heartfelt apology note, she'd asked Brisco to speak to Meidani for her. She'd gotten drunk and thrown some guy in the fountain for calling her a bitch. She was running out of ways to embarrass herself, but failing at a simple cleanup could do it.

She'd lost Meidani, but she would not lose her touch. Getting paid was the one thing she'd been doing right for ten-plus years.

There weren't many places left to check for the remnants of this blob infestation, and they were all unlikely, but she was going into space to check them. She wanted the money, but more than that, she needed to pretend her life wasn't a complete failure.

Anelace started pulling on a poorly jointed pressure suit she'd liberated from a life raft on the abandoned lower decks of the station. It was a muddy brown-black color with long strips of fluorescent orange up the limbs. The clasps were clunky and the feet were a painful auto-fit contraption. But hey, it kept air in your lungs and eyeballs in your head.

Anelace checked her list on the counter again—full air, suit on and sealed, air filters running, mask in place. She triggered the suits pressurizer and stood still while it whirred and puffed. It slowly inflated each segmented compartment, and checked for leaks. When the suit passed its self-inspection, it projected a cheerful green icon on the smoky plas-glass of the visor.

Anelace turned and walked the suit down the hall, adjusting to the oily swinging motion of assisted joints. The courier ship had two airlocks, and one was currently fused to the long arm of a station berth. She headed for the other airlock, wanting a door into empty space for the first time in her life.

Inside, she hesitated.

The room was surprisingly large, built to accommodate a cargo shunt. It was perfectly round, the walls dotted with plastic honeycomb grates. There were no windows into space beyond.

She clipped carabiners to herself in two places and hooked a line to the inside of the airlock. She tugged to verify, before pulling out a second line. Alone and ready in the airlock, Anelace raised her glove and pressed the big mechanical button mounted by the door.

There are three standard ways to die in space. The first, and most common way to die, was by being a dumbass and getting yourself crushed by a ship, cargo, or ship system. The second way to die was asphyxiation or cold temperatures—you tore a hole, had a suit failure, or lost track of time. The third way to die terrified her the most: accidental directional momentum. It was spacer-speak for losing hold and floating off, watching safety grow further and further in the distance. The suit came with an emergency puff of compressed gas, one last shot at pointing yourself in the right direction, but after that, you floated.

It would be her first spacewalk, so she'd read a how-to guide that morning in her quarters. It was a far difference from the recommended thirty-hour safety course and two experienced spotters, but finding an experienced spacewalker would be complicated, and blow her take.

Chirp?

An electronic noise asked for confirmation. A bright panel on the wall, an eight-inch square of smoky crystal, warned of danger with a stylized illustration of blood flying from a man's major orifices.

She pressed the button again.

Chirp.

The panel changed to a gauge with a thick light for every 10% of progress. Oxygen was sucked back into the ship's systems with a hum she could feel in her feet. Very slowly, the pressure in the airlock dropped. As the gauge crept below the 60% range, she felt the suit lifting away, pulled by vacuum.

Chirp?

Anelace tugged at her tether one last time, and pressed the button again.

The outer door irised open, wide metal teeth rotating and retracting into the wall. Stars twinkled cold in the distance. It was the same view you got from the station, but there was nothing between her and the infinity. The lack of a window made an everyday view terrifying.

The strip of lighting along her helmet flickered on. It didn't dent the eternal darkness. Her blood was chilled in her veins, but her heartbeat too fast. The next step would be the hardest.

If she made herself go out there, and didn't find the infestation, she was going to firebomb this gut-eating ship.

She tugged again at her tether, closed her gloved hand tight around it. The gloves were bulky—everything was bulky. It was hard to believe she had a good grip when she couldn't feel what she held.

Anelace took one last glance at space, still dark and foreboding, still wondrous and eternal, and cussed softly. Then she stepped close to the door, closed her eyes and eased her left leg out.

A few inches outside, the downward pull of artificial gravity turned inward before disappearing altogether. Her reflexes went wild—she was falling! She was broken!

Anelace stood perfectly still, one leg out the door like a crazy bird, until the moment passed. Then she wrapped her body around the curved lip of the opening, one hand on an inside handle, the other on an outside handle.

She'd seen videos of spacers swarming over ships, bounding along, relying on a tether and skill. Would she be bounding? Oh hell no.

She eased the rest of the way out, finding another handhold. There were three handles to help her climb outside. She exhausted them quickly. She side-climbed one more rung, and attached a second tether. Her eyes fluttered open, but the sight of stars beyond her toes, a smooth hull in front of her, froze her in place.

Don't panic.

She tightened her grip until it hurt, just clinging. Her stomach felt like it was bouncing around in her abdomen.

Too late.

The only thing keeping her from being sick was two injections, a round of pills, and a patch behind her ear. You could shake her like a jammed auto-door and she wouldn't puke.

Anelace pressed a gloved hand directly to the hull. Gravity grabbed it, like metal against a weak magnet, a nice side effect of reverse directional gravity drives. She lifted her hand and moved it higher on the ship, pulling herself along in a crawl. Okay, that was good. Her research hadn't been wrong, so far.

She could see part of the station. Even at the end of a quarter-mile long docking arm, she was too close to see all of it.

Her home was a hulking mass in the approximate shape of a giant metal hairball, crisscrossed with conduits and protrusions over an off-center sphere. She was looking at the widest part of the lump, the docks, where dozens of arms extended short and long for ships to berth on. It wasn't elegant, and it looked much larger than it felt while living on it.

And she still had to find some blobs.

"No problem," she muttered, talking to herself like a true crazy person.

With a grin she couldn't shut down on her face, she started crawling up. Happiness came and went, but adrenaline highs were forever.

There were eighteen places she wanted to check, areas carefully chosen from the ship's plans: water ports, fuel ports, air ports, waste ports, mechanical access and towing hooks. All were supposedly sealed. All of them seemed likely candidates for a contamination that even her thorough cleanings didn't reach.

She still wore her first tether—the lifeline. She'd feed it out from her waist, letting it float in space and wrap the hull behind her. She secured a second tether, short and thick, into a connector in the hull made for it.

When she got going, movement across the outside of the ship came easier than she expected. If she could just remember she had to point her face at an area for it to be illuminated by her helmet lights, she'd be set. With a hex key on a retractable string, she opened access panels for the different areas she was checking.

By the time she hit the fifth port on her list, she was on a roll. She was high on the ship, halfway around to the station berth. The access plate gave a little pop onto hinges, and she pushed a well-oiled plate of metal out of the way. It slid upward on frictionless rollers.

She pushed the plate higher, impatiently exposing the complicated valve of a water port lurking underneath.

Droplets appeared in a loose pattern across her visor—a spray of liquid across her front. She moved her hand up to wipe, but paused. That would make it worse. Then she noticed more droplets on her hand, thin liquid turned into quivery little bumps by surface tension. And then she realized it probably wasn't water.

Her breath hissed between her teeth, the long slow exhale between realization and stark horror.

The water port was made to be fail proof. It hadn't been leaking under the panel, or it'd have torn open further. There was no such thing as a harmless pinpoint leak in faster than light travel.

She reached out with the hex key, scraping it along the channels of the water valve. Then she poked it into the recess under the edges of the maintenance panel, the dark empty space between hull plates.

A two-inch nucleus floated free, perfectly formed. The blob had been torn apart by the plate, helped by vacuum. It would regenerate eventually, with moisture—only fire could truly kill the devil-blessed ball suckers.

Anelace let it float away, considering the dots on her field of view. Would this kill her?

She ignored the remaining ports. She forgot the money. Instead, she headed back the way she came, making for the airlock. She pushed her sideways crawl to the limit, faster and faster. Adrenaline warred with her careful movements, making her feel ill. Changing tether ports took too long, so she strained against the elastic of the short line, reaching twice as far before securing it again.

The suit was a strong polycarbon composite, the cheapest sold for escape suits, but still called indestructible. Anelace expected it to stand up to the ichor of a blob for at least ten minutes. Maybe.

The airlock yawned wide in front of her, ringed by lights. Safety. She hooked her elbow to firmly grasp the last handle, slid a knee and foot to rest on the deck. Her climb back into the ship was much faster than the climb out had been. Where her arm slid on the hull, it left behind a faint smear of flesh-eating fluid.

She wobbled a step into the round room, and turned back to the wide view of space. The stars were harsh, uncaring witness to her situation.

She smacked the lone button beside the airlock door. The door slowly irised shut. She controlled her breathing, appeasing the suit.

There were cloudy spots with little white outlines under the liquid on the visor now. It hadn't penetrated, not yet, but the tiny droplets of liquid had begun to etch the composite.

She looked down and took a careful visual inventory of her suit; she didn't touch, didn't smear ichor, just looked.

The suit was badly discolored where splashed, faded to an ashen grey. It looked fragile. And droplets had started to trickle downward, now affected by gravity. There was a long arc of grey dots near her knee. There was a big spot of grey on her left mid torso. There was a big swath of droplets across her right chest, up, as far as she could see, probably up her neck and across her visor.

The airlock door pressed shut, but pressure did not flood back. The progress gauge appeared on the panel near the door, starting at 5%.

Anelace closed her eyes, and imagined she could feel time itself slowing down. Her breath felt like sludge in her lungs.

She already knew her plan. She'd wait until the panel flickered green and she'd carefully get out of this suit. Once a leak wasn't a worry, she had time. Ichor would make it to her skin eventually, but not in a hurry. The suit was damn tough.

She stood ramrod straight, hands clenched, with her eyes closed, trying to sense a leak, but that was disaster. Her breathing sped, her thoughts raced. If she hyperventilated, she only made things worse. If she fainted here, she would die, and after years of taunting death, that would just be embarrassing.

The gauge on the wall was still a bright red color, a lighted stack of bars filled about forty percent. If she opened her helmet, she probably wouldn't smear like a bug, but she might rupture her eardrums and stir fry her brain a bit.

She stared harder—it was the only thing she could do. The status panel crept up, past sixty percent, and turned orange-yellow. Well, that was better than red.

Anelace looked away—and her gaze caught on a flickering color shift, low, near the wall. There was a blob in the airlock with her. Her hand fell to her belt, but no weapon met her grasp. That belt—the belt she needed for dealing with blobs—was under the suit. It's not like you could start a fire in space, right?

She turned in a slow circle, assessing the threat. Two blobs were on the ground, creeping toward her. Both were oddly shriveled, their normally taut hide creased with wrinkles. A larger one was above them, squeezing with agonized slowness through a vent.

A hole opened in her suit with a faint wind of escaping air. She could feel it stir her sweat-soaked clothing. The suit lost the subtle tension of pressurization.

Belatedly, a red warning icon projected on the inside of her visor. It showed the universal wavy lines of an air leak, which told her nothing she didn't already know, and obscured her view.

She took a deep breath, reminding herself that she could. An uncomfortable gasket around her neck allowed the helmet to be pressurized higher than the suit, to protect her ears and sinuses. It was a separate compartment from her torso.

She turned in another circle, confirming the positions of the three blobs. The one was still wiggling obscenely in the vent, the other two pulsing in slow motion.

The gauge on the wall was up to eighty percent.

She unclipped her suit gloves and dropped them to the floor grate. Then she freed her feet. She had to beware the blob juice on the suit, but needed to undress quickly, too.

The blobs on the ground were strange, wizened and listing. But maybe not completely impaired. Soon, they would register her presence.

And then searing agony took a bite out of her. She doubled over, her bare hands clutching at her abdomen. Her skin tried to crawl away from the pain, her muscles cramping and pulling against her tender gut. She was too late. The acid was through the suit.

After a second to regroup, her will took over. She flexed her fingers then focused on getting free. She clawed apart the suit's final seam and tugged the shapeless bulk off her shoulders.

As the suit fell away, her pain changed. Her body spasmed, and she fell screaming to the deck. She didn't know where her injury was, just that pain was everything. It swamped her mind and stole her breath. It was a force she could barely comprehend.

This time, she might die. She knew it, but she couldn't give up. She had to save this. Meidani couldn't know she'd screwed up again.

She gritted her teeth until she could taste enamel, and drug herself a few more inches. Finally, she was free of the suit. And she kept crawling, further from the blobs, closer to the door.

Chirp?

The gauge glowed a green 100%, but the button near the ship's entrance was high, meant for someone standing. Survival had been reduced to simple motions, to breathing, to standing. She imagined strength as a water fountain, burbling up, and used it to pull herself the last few feet.

She pressed that mockingly cheerful button with a hand twisted into a claw of pain.

The blobs were closer now. They were fixed on her, creeping in her direction. Three small, loopy blobs, and they could finish her off easily.

The door back into the ship slid open.

The pain was dulling, falling into a weightless roar at the back of her mind. It was a relief, but it was disturbing. Was the acid past the skin, past the nerves? Her shoulders wouldn't raise. Her back only responded for some motions.

She got the popper from her belt with one nearly strengthless hand, and she fired it, again and again, surrounding the blobs in a barrage of kerosene. Then she fell forward, trying to walk through the door, but not able to bend like that.

She pushed herself a few feet more, tumbling to her back and screaming into the depths of the empty ship. But she wasn't done.

Above her, the door stood open. A bright green button glowed beside it.

The hallway would be clear of blobs. The ones chasing her from the airlock were part of the hull infestation, stirred up by Anelace opening port hatches. She just had to close the airlock.

She pulled her laser free, prying it out from under her torso. The blobs had crossed the room, far too close to her crumpled body. But they were still slow. They were still in the airlock.

Her hand was shaking. She aimed, badly, through the wide open door, steadied herself, aimed again. She fired the laser with careful precision. She didn't have to hit the blobs, but it'd be nice if she didn't shoot herself in the leg.

A few breaths of steady pressure on the trigger, and a fire started. An impish little blaze rapidly spread in the puddle of accelerant.

She let her head fall to the grating, just for a second.

The fire warning started. It was a loud booming klaxon that reminded her of Meidani, and that night in the Olive Branch. The sound thudded through her brain.

A fire door slammed down, blocking the doorway to the airlock and slicing messily through the nearest blob. It blocked the way for the other two. Anelace was safe.

But her ankle screamed a new agony, lower than the pain she was growing used to. She'd been splashed by more ichor... she'd...

She slipped into the grace of unconsciousness.

TEN

Anelace woke in dim light, tucked into a hazy bed. Her thoughts were a lazy ribbon winding through her mind. She looked around, but her head didn't move, so she couldn't see much.

The walls were close, the bed low, the light had a blue paper shade. It was her bed. But the sheets were the crisp white bedding of a hospital.

Her eyelids drifted downward. She hurt, deeply, but it was odd pain; it made her want to sleep. The darkness behind her closed eyes was pleasant, like a good hug.

She was drugged. Her thoughts still floated, but she realized this wasn't the first time she'd woken.

The details of her near death were there, but hard to grasp all at once. How had she survived? How was she in her own quarters? And how long had she been there?

A sob drifted through the open door, and Anelace's mind floundered to identify it. When the answer came, a new sort of pain the drugs couldn't cushion stabbed her.

Meidani was crying.

Anelace opened her mouth, but all that came was a croak. Her voice was lost to disuse. She reached up a hand, and it was an ordeal she didn't anticipate. The movement sparked pain, pulling muscles in a way that woke other pain.

The medication grabbed her in its teeth, dragging her toward darkness, but she fought back. She refused to sleep while Meidani cried.

The tip of her fingers found a bandage at the base of her throat, an injury she didn't remember or understand. How? She let her body relax for just a second, to let herself think. Unconsciousness chased her under.

The next time she opened her eyes, it was still dim. Her sheets were still crisp and white. Her body still felt like a beaten pile. Pain medication was still sludge in her veins.

She didn't move. She didn't fight the drugs, or fight the pain either. She would try to ride it.

She could hear Meidani. Her voice drifted in from the other room.

"Mother, I'm perfectly fine. It's safe here. And she needs me." Meidani's tone was carefully respectful. That was the appropriate voice to use when disagreeing with her mother.

Meidani's voice paused.

"No, I know. I know we're not. But she needs me. I have to be here. She can't be alone, and she can't stay in the med ward without getting arrested."

A longer pause.

"I promise. We're not back together. She's not even awake."

They weren't together. Anelace couldn't decide if their breakup or their time together felt more like a dream.

Anelace drifted behind her closed eyes some more, but she didn't think she slept.

Then she was jarred awake by a little broken sound. Meidani was crying again. Anelace heard a breath and a sniffle and more pain than she knew how to cope with.

Anelace's eyes opened. Meidani was in a chair near the door arch, a scanner in her hand. She was perfectly neat, her blouse pressed and every hair of her braid in place, but there were deep bags under her eyes and she had a wan, translucent look to her.

Tears ran slowly down Meidani's face, though she barely made a sound.

"No," Anelace croaked. "I'm okay."

"Don't talk. You'll make it worse." Meidani fiercely wiped at her cheek. "And your idea of okay is horrible."

"I'm an idiot. Don't cry."

"You are an idiot."

"Please..."

"Shut up!"

Anelace gulped, a bad idea. She paused, and was escorted back into sleep by the unyielding command of her pain medication.

Anelace stared at her bedroom ceiling again. She'd memorized it during the last six weeks of healing—the only thing she'd seen more of was the fleshy inside of her own eyelids.

After her near death, she'd had a tracheotomy, muscle grafting along her left foot and leg, two fingers on her right hand had been removed, a few of her vertebrae and some of her intestines replaced with synthetic, and large swathes of nerve-dead skin removed and flash-healed. But her deepest injury was her guilt. She finally understood what her choices could do to Meidani. She'd seen the worst, as Meidani stopped crying but turned wan, and she'd been helpless to stop it.

Today, she was going to fix it. Somehow.

Anelace disentangled from the sheets slowly and rose with care and a little cursing. She steadied herself with a shoulder on the wall before shuffling toward the sleeping cubby's entrance.

She wasn't being a complete idiot. Meidani had helped her test her healing every day, physical therapy getting more intense as she could take it. This wasn't the first time she'd stood; it was just the one time it wasn't on the doc's orders.

She felt pain on standing, of course, but nothing serious. Worse, her body felt wrong. New muscle was strong enough to hold her, but she'd lost flexibility. Her back and her leg didn't respond as quickly as it once had. Her reflexes were a bitter memory.

She needed the conversations that Meidani had been avoiding. She needed to ask the questions Meidani had staved off by being unnaturally talkative, or walking into the other room. Who found her? What about Meidani's job at the No Name? How had Meidani convinced the station doc to do so much work on Anelace without reporting it to station governance?

She was mobile now. Meidani couldn't run anymore.

Anelace walked out to find Meidani bent over a rucksack. At Meidani's feet was a pile of folded clothing, an extra pair of shoes, some electronics. She was fully dressed, wearing a golden brown tunic that flattered the beauty of her skin. Though Anelace knew Meidani had been sleeping in the living room, there was no sign of bedding.

When the other woman saw it was Anelace, her face closed down. Meidani had a great poker face.

"You're leaving?"

"You should be in bed."

Anelace's legs already felt like a burnt pudding—a little too firm, but wobbly in the center. She leaned against the door arch as nonchalantly as she could. It wasn't enough, but she would out-stubborn this like she'd out-stubborned everything else in her life.

"Anelace, you need to sit down."

"I'll sit, if you'll talk to me. But if you leave, I'm going to chase you."

Meidani sighed. It was a sound of exhausted patience and a little nostalgia, like she missed Anelace's teasing.

Anelace pressed harder. "I really will do it. I'll chase you down the hall."

"You'll fall on your face, and I won't stop to fix you this time. I have limits."

Limits... Right. Meidani's limits were stunted. If Anelace could go back in time and give her some, she would, so Anelace could never have hurt her so badly. But time travel was science fiction, and Anelace was too desperately selfish to let her go now.

"Would you stay? If I begged?" Anelace asked.

Anelace hated herself. She almost wanted the woman she loved to tell her to go to hell.

Meidani's poker face crumbled around the edges.

"Not to take care of me," Anelace clarified. "I can find someone to change sheets. But see me, please. Let me take you to tea. Let me take you for tequila shots and table dancing."

Meidani's expression firmed, but a tear leaked from her eye.

"I can't. I'm sorry. I know you don't understand, but I just can't."

"I do understand."

Meidani shook her head. A strand of jet hair lay across her cheek, catching falling tears.

"Come here."

"You need to sit."

"I'll sit if you sit in my lap."

Meidani snorted, a snotty noise. She wasn't a pretty crier.

Anelace's leg spasmed, and reminded her Meidani was always right. Anelace did need to sit. She clutched the door arch and lowered herself to the floor, against the wall.

Meidani walked nearer, torn between worry and resolve.

"I'm fine. I just need a second." Anelace looked down, baiting a trap.

When she'd lured Meidani close enough, she reached out with her good hand and grabbed the standing woman's pant leg.

"Sit with me."

Meidani shook her head no, but she sat. She sat close to Anelace and buried her head against her shoulder. She wound a hand into Anelace's, touching her for comfort for the first time since that stupid bar fight.

That touch felt like sunlight on snow looked. It was warmth and hope and somehow made everything harsh. The wisps of hair gently nestled against Anelace's cheek were angel kisses.

With that hand in hers, Anelace forgot the words she'd been practicing all morning, so she came up with new ones. "I've been bad for you, I know, but you need me. I need you. I know I should find a nice boy for you, some steady guy to settle down with. But it wouldn't feel this way if we weren't meant for each other."

Anelace felt Meidani's throat move against her arm.

"I do understand. I'm sorry I've been so horrible for you. I'm so sorry."

Meidani squeezed her hand and interrupted. "I can't. I can't worry about you, every day, every time you're out of my sight. But I know who you are; I wouldn't ask you to change yourself just because I can't handle it."

"Please ask me to change. I will. I promise." Meidani's shoulders shook, but she made no sound. "I don't make promises lightly. You know that. You asked around, right? I don't promise any woman anything. But I promise, if you'll just let me convince you, I'll stay safe. No more risks."

"I want to believe you, but I know better. You're addicted to danger. That look on your face, the way you get, that's addiction. If you could stop risking your life for stupid reasons, you would have by now."

"I'm addicted to you, Meidani, if anything. I know this sounds like the same thing again; I'm asking for another chance when you've given me a dozen. But I didn't understand before. I understand now. I won't do it again. If I did, you're done. You can send your brothers to beat me up."

Meidani refused to laugh. "That is also missing the point."

"A joke."

Anelace stroked her two remaining fingers through Meidani's hair, silk on callouses. She couldn't lift her arm higher to reach Meidani's face.

"I'll be the safest person on the station. I could get a job in maintenance, and do this the hands off way, with bots and section decontaminations. Or I could find something else. Waitress. Or..."

Anelace racked her brain for safe jobs on this giant rat's nest and came up short. Office jobs were rare, and Anelace could barely read anyway.

"Okay. You get one shot. Okay?" Meidani said it in her sternest voice, warming the depths of Anelace's heart.

Anelace softly kissed Meidani's temple. Meidani turned her face up, a total mess. Anelace kissed her properly, if lightly. The light brush against Anelace's rough lips was relief poured over pain. It felt like bliss. Like hope.

When they broke the kiss, Anelace saw hope in Meidani's eyes as well. It was a hope she vowed not to crush.

"Can you get yourself back into bed?" Meidani asked.

Anelace hesitated.

"No?" Meidani said.

"Probably not."

"You idiot. I'm going to have to call Brisco to lift you. I can't do it yet."

"Is he going to drop me on purpose?"

Finally, Meidani smiled. She smiled a sincere, forgiving, wonderful, if sad, smile. "Maybe."

"I could sleep on the floor," Anelace suggested. Her own smile kinda hurt. Did those muscles atrophy?

"No," Meidani said firmly. "You idiot."

She snuggled closer to Anelace and Anelace snuggled back. The contact felt so good. Anelace felt so content to just sit there with her.

"Mmhmm. I'm an idiot," Anelace agreed.

EPILOGUE

"I'm going to need you to give yourself up, no funny stuff. I don't want any trouble, Sir, and you don't want any either." Anelace drawled.

She peered into a mangled maintenance hatch near the floor, at the edge of the park area. Slats were missing, leaving just enough space for a twice-cussed kitten to wander in.

"How did you get in there, anyway?"

Meidani answered for him. "We were walking, and Minki got tangled in the harness. And when I tried to fix it, he got out."

Meidani was standing behind Anelace, on real grass beside a real dead tree. The nature park four levels below the promenade was rundown, but Meidani found it relaxing. And the blob problem this far in was fully under control, now.

Anelace used a pocketknife to loosen the second side of the grate, prying slowly, trying not to scare the thing deeper.

Of course, it was hissing at her like she was the Devil walking amongst god-fearing folk.

The grate fell away, and the kitten took a swipe. Anelace yanked her hand back.

"Hey! That's not nice. You know I'm not allowed to get injured. That's a dirty game."

"Oh, save me. You're bigger than him. Just get my cat."

The hissing found a new extra-menacing pitch.

"The cat hates me."

Her wife just laughed.

Anelace pulled gloves from her belt and slid them on her hands. She flexed her right hand, the stiff one, but today was a good day.

Then she struck without warning, swooping in on the cat before it could draw deeper into the crawl space.

The cat meeped and tried to jump. Anelace caught it midair. The kitten sunk tiny claws into the hand holding it, and Anelace turned, holding the vicious bundle of fluff at arm's length.

Meidani came up to take her cat, which promptly turned into a purring love-beast. It snuggled up to Meidani's chest and tucked itself into the crook of her elbow.

"You're gullible. It has you completely fooled," Anelace observed.

Meidani's smile quirked. Her beauty turned into radiance with just a hint of attitude. Anelace stared, a wave of awe goosing her senses.

Meidani stepped closer. Her hand fell naturally to her side, extending to meet Anelace's.

"Were you injured?" Meidani asked the question she asked every day when Anelace got home from work.

"No, ma'am. Not a scratch." And that was the usual answer.

"I suppose I'll keep you a while longer, then."

"What about the cat?"

"Be nice to the cat."

"I'm nice! Why isn't he?"

"He's just jealous because he thinks I like you better."

Meidani smiled, and Anelace stepped closer. Meidani's lips were smooth, pink. Anelace kissed her softly, tracing the curve of her lip with her own.

An angry claw sank into her breast, breaking tender flesh.

"Holy devil's spawn in a pretty pink dress," Anelace cussed.

Meidani just laughed at her and led the way home.

Thank You

Thank you for reading *Hellcat's Bounty*. I hope you enjoyed it as much as I've enjoyed writing and releasing it.

What Next?

This is only the first entry in the Rosewood world. I'm currently hard at work on the sequel: another story of life, danger and two women falling in love on Rosewood, a forgotten backsystem space station. The next book will feature a new couple, and be novel length.

Acknowledgments

A giant, bubbling, gooey bowl of thanks to the wonderful people I'm surrounded by. They give me advice, support, and inspiration on a daily basis. My Twitter people are more rare and wonderful and awe-inspiring and glittery than unicorn poop.

Thank you to Laurie for your input on this manuscript at nearly every meal we've shared for the last year, the borrowing of your amazing analytical mind, and for your days of work in the final push. Thank you to Karina for your voice of wisdom (first time you've gotten that one?), your unfailing encouragement, and for the amaaazing blurb. Thank you to Cathy for an experienced voice of encouragement when I really fucking needed it. And thank you Kanaxa and Rhonda for your hard work on the final product.

And an extra side of thank you to every person who has greeted news of "the lesbian space western" with curiosity and eagerness. It has meant the world to me.

Also by Renae Jones

Taste of Passion (straight scifi romance, Carina Press)

Made in the USA
Lexington, KY
04 April 2019